T0146980

VESTIGE

JOSETH MOORE

authorHOUSE®

AuthorHouse™
1663 Liberty Drive
Bloomington, IN 47403
www.authorhouse.com
Phone: 1 (800) 839-8640

Published by AuthorHouse 09/25/2019

ISBN: 978-1-7283-2862-1 (sc)
ISBN: 978-1-7283-2863-8 (e)

Library of Congress Control Number: 2019914788

Print information available on the last page.

CONTENTS

To my wife and love of my
life, Deni; our three children,
and the generations after
them...and to the Earth.

CHAPTER ONE

Tyra Housenn's internal, cerebral message from her supervisor, Mirandana, auto-connected while Tyra unloaded her vehicle that had dropped her off at the big, old and rusty door to that particular section of the generation-Ship. Big, as in, it was about the size of a two-storey edifice that one would see in the old residential district of the Ship!

Tyra's self-actuator vehicle, with its canopy in lock-down mode, flashed lights and made some audibles to signify to the woman in her twenties that it was about to park off to the side and the human needed to give it some space so she would not get run-over!

"Mirandana, are you *sure* this is where the contractor wants me to check for that signal?" By this time, Tyra had finished unpacking her necessary equipment for her maintenance job. She glanced at one of her info-tools. "By stars' gravity, this portal is so old, it doesn't even register as having been serviced by *any* of the contractors since—"

"Launch date of the Ship," the older woman said over their cerebral-comm. "Yeah, I did a little research on it before the business had me send you over... If you have trouble getting it open, request succor from the synthetics."

Tyra tsked sarcastically. "We have some explosives that'll do the job!"

A shared laugh...

"The Company has allotted your

payments for a full day's worth—*maximum*, Tyra. So, don't get in too much of a hurry where you hurt yourself *or* damage the ship, affirmed?"

The Ship-maintenance crewmember wasn't quite finished yet. "If it's so important, why are they having a main-tech search for this signal? Shouldn't some official from one of the engineering schemes do this?"

Tyra could see over the cerebral-comm that her boss showed some apprehension, despite herself. But she merely shrugged. "Corporation gods don't tell me the details...I'm guessing they have a lot of bigger projects they have to deal with—like making sure our home-Ship doesn't run out of energy. Or making sure we can withstand the *next* meteor storm! To *them*, sending engineering over to look for some unexpected signal deep in the *original* sector of the Ship would be a little too much like playing archaeology..."

"Digging a little *too* deep in history, is it," Tyra quipped as she approached the towering slab of the pitted and dusty metallic door. Various layers of texts and labels from long-ago generations had intermittently graffitied the portal. "And you've wondered why I've never dated an engineer!"

A chuckle from her over-visor. "I'm guessing it's just some ancient proximate-reader for a business that's long-dead."

That caused Tyra to pause in her tracks. "But to read *what*? However long it's been since our Ship voyaged out of our solar system and got barnacled with asteroids, our ancestors had no idea *where* they were going...so why would they need a proximate-timer?"

"Like I said—*too much archaeology for the engineers*...that's why we have *you* there!"

The main-tech shook her head. "Stars, I love a mystery! Ok, boss; message received...I previously checked all messaging and visuals to ensure functionality parameters are standard, and same goes for my synth-tools and computerables..."

"Ok, that's an affirmed—contact me *directly* if something weird happens!"

And their implanted comms were disengaged.

One Hour Later...

Tech-Housenn was finally getting to the point where the heavy, house-sized door was beginning to shutter from all her synthetic-labors' work of using heat with some oils to get the port sliding! That is, *after* she had programmed her synths to scrape away at all the rust that had cemented the door!

"Tech-Housenn," one of the synthetics had audioed over the shrieking of metal scraping against metal as the port nudged, "it is recommended that only five feet is needed for you to passage the port!"

She gave a terse nod. "That would be the most logical approach," she said over the noise as the other synthetic labors continued to coat the threshold of the huge portal with industrial grease as their mechanical grappling arms forced the looming door to open. Again, just a few feet.

And suddenly, there was silence after the synths finished moving the door... Silence, but for a faint gust of humid, stuffy air that escaped the other side of that time capsule!

While she was reading her portable

computerized equipment, Tyra barked out telemetry for the recording. "Oxygen has been slightly burned up in there—nineteen percent; nitrogen, *eighty* percent...carbon dioxide approaching *two-tenths of a percent*!...methane just short of *thirty-thousandths*!"

Tyra ponderously looked up from her reader and peered into the darkened side of the portal while the recording kept going. Her computerable device interjected the obvious.

"Tech-Housenn, something has been *using* the air during the eon *since* the commencement of the Ship's voyage!"

Silence...more moistened air breezing by the main-tech and her small synthetic crew...

"That's impossible!"

"Apparently not," one of the

boxy, somewhat anthropomorphic, synthetics said dryly.

"Synths," Tyra put to her three mechanicals, "would *now* be a good time to contact Supervisor Ellisante? She said to do so—*directly*—if we ran into anything weird...I would classify this as weird!"

Surprisingly, there was a pause among the synths!

"Perhaps it would help if we were to scan for any life forms *first*," one of the synths volunteered. "With such a vast space vehicle, it is possible that an enclosed section within the Ship *could* usurp the original air that was contained after your ancestors decided to close off this section of the Ship."

There was a series of audibles from Tyra's portable device. "Tech-Housenn, I took advantage of your conversation and scanned for life signs and have found *none*—with the exception of mere traces of micro-organisms that normally reside in an urban ecosystem dominated by humans."

She frowned; slightly relaxing her tense posture. "So, basically, no life signs?"

"That is correct," the portable responded.

"Tech-Housenn," another of the three synths input, "it is possible that the aggregate-effects of such germs are responsible for the relatively off-kilter readings; especially over such vast amounts of time."

There was a chorus of, '*Indeed,*' between the two other synths and the tech's portable device!

This caused Tyra to feel a lot better, as she nodded to herself. "Affirmed, then...I say we go locate that proximate-timer and get this job done!"

More synthetic affirmations from the synths and her portable. All the synths turned on a built-in light that each harbored; flooding the immediate area behind the portal with electrifying light! But a few seconds after the mechanical laborers and the human stepped through the grand portal, Tyra had a thought as she looked back at the partially opened door behind them.

"I don't care which one of you, but I'd like one of you synths to stand guard on the *other* side of the portal... you never know when an emergency might come up and *one* of us should be on the *outside* of that gigantic door!"

Without a word, one of the synths simply turned and smoothly gaited toward the slit of light coming through the portal's hatch...

As the rest of the team cautiously walked further into the cavernous section—the light cast from the two remaining laborers—Tyra finally got to *see* just how *big* the enclosed section of her generational Ship was...Tyra's portable had already scanned the entire sector: well over a million square-feet! One of the synths projected a three-dimensional rendering of the layout of the sector, demarking where the search team was at each second. The overall design of the sector was a bit irregular, in shape. A multitude of compartmentalization—from rooms the size of a simple abode to caverns about a third of that one million square-feet! And as big as that was, main-tech Tyra had to remind herself that the closed-off sector was merely *one-fifth* of the entire generation-Ship that they all were passengers on...

Not surprisingly, the very cultural *feel* of that sector of the generational ship was from a vastly *different* era from Tyra Housenn's generation. Indeed, while they continued to search for the enigmatic signal, Tyra, the two remaining synths, and her portable device, *all* had pointed out from time to time the various spots where they could see how Tyra's ancestors had constructed and expanded upon the original Ship's layout.

Some parts the small team could tell where the very conception of the Ship itself—the infrastructure and superstructure looked more jumbled with rivers of conduit pipes, perhaps, a hundred feet across *each*! And as one looked back *toward* the giant portal, where the search team came from, they were able to tell there were several more years of advanced technology by the time the ancestors had built the looming portal!

How the ancients of Tech-Housenn's people did this, even the synths and the portable computerable had no viable reference to.

Which, of course, led to the obvious question that needed to be spoken aloud...

"So, why would my ancestors close this sector off from the rest of the Ship," Tyra put out to any of the computerables.

"And also, Tech-Housenn," her portable said, "about what timeline did they do this? We've been in this cordoned sector for a while, now, and I've yet to see *any* signs of a conflict or an emergency..."

All went quiet as they thought on the questions that were just posed. And then—

"Tech-Housenn," one of the synths exclaimed; it's boxy figure quickly swiveled toward another section of the cavern, "I've got the signal!"

"Good job...could you take us there?"

"Ma'am!" Using one of the benefits in being a synthetic being, the synth snapped out wheels from beneath its feet and quickly rolled toward where it had found the signal! The other synth of the search party had done the same with its wheels. The human hurried behind both the best she could; her light source emanating from her portable!

The two synths rolled straight into a relatively small section that would've been considered a "suite" in ancient times. There were no doors, so it was easy access for all to start looking around the collection of rooms...

"Right here, Tech-Housenn!" This was the other synth.

The two synthetics and the human all converged upon some ancient form of a console. Impossibly, the only instrument working in all the ruins was that flashing, alternating colorful light!

"I suggest touching it, someone," Tyra's portable prompted in the frozen awe!

One of the synths took the portable's suggestion... A high-pitched whirring sound followed and was gone in a few seconds. The flashing light on the console was the same colors, though it glowed a solid light now.

Suddenly, a flash of light winked on in front of them—startling the human! The two synths were surprised, but not startled as the biological being was next to them. That light originated from a large, rectangular surface; smooth and made of glass—or something similar. And within that lit rectangular, flat object were, unmistakably, letters! Indeed, words... Maintenance Tech Tyra Housenn had heard about such ancient systems of communicating before, when she was a little girl growing up in the rotating, cylindrical sector of the Ship. The ancients called such system Writings, or Words...

Accompanying the strange squiggles was a rather severe, flashing picture—an image, of some thin piece of line that was animated. As if that slender needle were quivering. And above *it*, in addition to that Writing, there were a series of, yet, smaller lines—a bit more blocky, and arranged in an arching fashion.

Tyra checked to make sure her visuals were still recording, and they were. "How curious!"

"...Tech-Housenn—" one of the synths started.

"—isn't this wonderful, everyone!" She flashed a smile and was truly giddy! "We are witnessing, in real-time, how the ancients communicated with each other! In *our* era, we've been using icono—"

"—Tech Housenn," this time, the other synthetic laborer tried.

"—and I'll send this experience today to the major societal journals... perhaps that's what our ancestors were doing when they abandoned this sector: keeping a kind of *reserve* for how—"

"—Maintenance Tech Housenn," her portable actually *yelled* at her! Obviously, the computerable had gotten her attention. "One of the things we, computerables—including your synths—are programmed for is some basic cultural information. Of course, from contemporary times to most of antiquities... This projection is a deeply disturbing message for *every* single being residing within the Ship..."

Just before Tyra could respond, one of the synths interjected. "Tech-Housenn, it translates into, *Running Low...*"

The maintenance tech *still* did not comprehend. "Low on what?"

"*Fuel,* Tech-Housenn," her portable came back in the dialogue. "Apparently, your ancestors had found some kind of fuel where a civilization could run off it for thousands of years."

"*Nuclear,* I believe is what they called it," the other synthetic input.

"Nuclear..." the human repeated, "nuclear—I've heard of it! In history, we studied how..."

Her eyes drifted to some corner of the chamber.

"Yes, Tech-Housenn," the portable said softly, "I think you've figured out and completed the task your contractor has given you...your ancestors used this nuclear to power this generational ship for an eon, but in doing so, there, apparently, was an accident. Ma'am, there was a very good reason *why* your ancestors closed off this sector from the rest of the Ship..."

Now, it was silent between the two synthetic beings, the portable computerable that was attached to Tyra's upper-left arm, and the young female human...silent except for the ancient electronic alarm—though no longer beeping since one of the synths had engaged the alarm button, but there was a constant *humm* in place.

"Radiation, Portable," she asked the

small device; half-way *not* wanting to hear the answer!

"That, Maintenance Tech Housenn, is actually the *good* news here, today... apparently so much time has gone by since whatever event it was that may have triggered your ancestors' abandonment of this sector, that the radiation levels are negligible! Though there are trace-amounts. I'd venture to suggest that we not stay here much longer, Tech-Housenn; just to be safe."

"Agreed!"

"Tech-Housenn," one of the two synthetic laborers asked as the team started to turn around to head back to the large portal, "are we to shut the door behind us? It would seem to be the most logic to do; given what we've learned here."

The young woman slightly flinched upon hearing the

question—apparently, she had not thought of that!

"That *would* be the obvious, precautionary thing to do, synth... synthetic Number Two," she called out over her comm-device to the mechanical that had voluntarily gone back to the portal to stand guard, "we're on our way back."

"Indeed, Tech-Housenn...I've been observing the reconnaissance team all this time. And I hope you don't mind, Maintenance Tech Housenn, but I've taken the liberty to contact Supervisor Ellisante of the mission. Including connecting the simultaneous-feed of the mission...by the time the four of you arrive, there should be a safety-evaluation crew here to look you all over for any radiation."

"Affirmed that, synth Two. And thank you..."

CHAPTER TWO

The Office of Infrastructure held an emergency meeting that same day, facilitated by one of the Ship's main self-actuator computerables; hours after Synthetic laborer Two had zipped Maintenance Technician Tyra Housenn's reconnaissance within the Ship's cordoned sector *to* Supervisor Mirandana Ellisante. It was not the entire employee-body of the Office, but of those who were in the major decision-making positions within the Ship.

Generations earlier, the charges of the Office of Infrastructure had the foresight to re-locate the agency within the middle section of the twenty-miles long spacecraft—that way the Office was equidistant from all sections of the Ship and travel-time was kept to a minimum! The *outer* hull of the Ship, Vestige, had *originally* been a smooth, elongated craft. But over the eon of its traversing outside Earth's solar system ended up being encrusted with meteors and asteroid debris.

However, given that Infrastructure was *not* located *within* the coveted O'Neillian cylinder sector of the Ship—mostly reserved for residential and more professionally academic zones, the Office had a bit of a low reputation...that their whole agency *was* maintenance, as opposed to maintenance being a division *within* the Infrastructure agency. With help from the Ship's myriad of science and engineering organizations *and* the Ship's own self-actuator, Infrastructure was the agency that *logistically* was the one in charge of maintaining that five-mile-wide, spinning colony of two-and-a-half or so *million* residents of the entire generational ship that people took for granted!

Given the centerpiece of the problem was the nuclear fuel that was powering the Ship had finally reached the threshold of minimal-operational levels, scores of scientists from various disciplines had, also, attended the emergency meeting. Since the current actuator computerable was a relatively new manufactured system programmed *by* much older systems some decades previously, it was the main reason *why* the Ship's systems were not aware of the nuclear fuel issue...in an ancient way of putting it:

nuclear energy being the very source of power *for* the island-sized ship was *Lost in Translation* during the reboot of the Ship's central systems those decades ago!

Even though she was considered low on the rung within Infrastructure, Main Tech Tyra Housenn, also, sat in on the meeting, as did her supervisor, Ellisante—*All Hands On Deck*, was another of the ancient aphorisms that was applicable.

The meeting, at that point, had been going on for about thirty minutes and scientists, engineers, and maintenance workers were *still* showing up—info devices on hand, as the late-comers pulled up a chair to the packed kiosk-tables, stationed close to each other...

"...twenty more years left," Maintenance Garson Hanway retorted; his head swiveling around as he looked at the large group around the different kiosk-tables. "By your cerebral-message, I thought we were about to sputter to a halt in a few *days*!"

Agreements were voiced around the media-tables...Tyra quietly noticed that *none* of them were from any of the scientists.

"Maintenance Hanway," Chemist Poul Ean replied in a bit condescending tone, "for a *generational* ship, we're fortunate to have had *this* much time to figure out how to deal with our fuel supply...as much time it takes for the logistics of trying to find the closest planet or moon for us to park next to and orbit; *then* you have to think about sending out scouting missions to those planets; and, of course, all the while we have to *keep* feeding and facilitating almost three *million* residents while we do this!"

"Indeed, Maintenance Hanway, twenty years is not a lot of time to deal with our dwindling ship-fuel," computerable physicist, Ellenain Eshe, put to the maintenance worker. She, then, turned her attention to the whole group at all the kiosk-tables—looking through projections of iconographic data that also depicted a diagram of the asteroid-encrusted ship at each table. (Ever since Tyra and her search team found that ancient signal, she had been more mindful how *her* generation communicated exclusively with pictographs. With the exception of math expressions.) "I'd like to hear from the Ship's rotating crew...You all know more than anyone else of the history the last time the Ship had made port on a planet or moon...whether or not we've had energy surges...I guess what I'm asking is, Do we have enough energy from this nuclear thing for us to even *look* for a planet to dock with and utilize *its* natural resources?"

"—Great question!"

"—Stars, we're in trouble if we even have to ask that!"

"—I heard a computerable report say something like a hundred years ago!"

"—Shouldn't that be in our records?"

"Ok, let's hear from the Ship's crew," Yeo, an engineer, suggested as she did a sweeping gesture with one of her hands.

The ancient ship's main crew were scattered among the other people at the kiosk-tables, but it was evident who they were by the way they glanced at one another to see who'd speak among them, *for* them.

Billamont Harvester, one of the Ship's rotating crew members, cleared his throat and, apprehensively, responded. "A few of us were discussing this while on the way here over our cerebral-comms...and you are actually on the point, Physicist Eshe, about the need to divert the Ship to an astronomic body in order to compensate our fuel-loss..."

"Why do I hear a, *But*, coming from you, Crew-Harvester," Astrophysicist Cairo an Preun pointed out from across the headquarters' conference hall. He kept his eyes on the shipmate while everyone else shifted in their respective seats to get a look at Billamont.

The shipmate's eyes uneasily flitted to his crewmates scattered around those media-tables before he responded. "Look, you can't expect a ship that started off with some thousands of residents thousands of years ago to ignore the issues related to *that* ship's fuel supply...years ago, we Crewmembers *did* discuss—more speculation, really—what we might have to do *should* the Ship run into some near-fatal incident with one of those meteor storms. Back then, when I was a new recruit, some of the elders suggested that we scrap our long-held philosophy of drifting about in space in a big ship and just *find* a habitable planet or moon to settle onto..."

There was a stir that began among some within the large meeting. Crew-Harvester went on.

"Well, like I said, it was more idle speculation than a serious policy to look into..." He shrugged, in a defeatist way, main tech Tyra noticed. "And that was pretty much it, sisters and brothers...it was kind of a sore spot to discuss this—almost political! Sadly, some of the crewmembers back in my young days as a shipmate wanted nothing to do with migrating to a planet or moon. I don't know...I guess one could've called them a kind of 'purist' movement within the Ship's crewmembers. You know; what's the point in constructing a generational ship just to dock it within a geo-centric orbit around, yet, another planet...?"

There were some tacit nods to that point, but the majority of the engineers, scientists, and even among the maintenance workers, were all looking upon Crew-Harvester with suspicious eyes! This was not lost on him.

"I guess the thrust of what I'm saying is, even though I, personally, was open to looking to settle onto a planet—and a few other crewmembers—the majority of the rotating crew were *not*! Between that mindset of the Ship's crew *and* our updated actuator systems *not* configuring the older systems with the programming of the nuclear fuel *with* them..." Now Crew-Harvester, in earnest, looked around at everyone in the conference hall, seated at those kiosk-tables. "*This* is how we got into this mess, apparently!"

For the first time of the emergency meeting, there was a ruckus!

"I ask that all in attendance please be respectful and keep all interactions courteous," the Ship's synthetic voice sternly put; its audible booming above. No doubt, there was some psychology at play in such gesture!

"You realize we've passed *two* planets since you've been a recruit, Crew-Harvester," maintenance tech

Bennie Dotansk put to all the rotating shipmates as she looked around the gathering.

There was a chorus of consent, as the attendees tried measuring their responses after the warning from the Ship's actuator!

"What's the next planet the Ship will run across," Geologist Fillip Natsome threw out to anyone.

"We've been in the periphery of the Canis Major Dwarf minor-galaxy for the past three years now," the Ship's actuator answered before any human scientists had a chance of even thinking on the subject! "During the era when the Ship was originally constructed, humans did not know a lot of details of the Virgo Supercluster, much less the planets *within* those galaxies..."

Just then, the Ship's actuator changed the projected iconographics hovering above the center of each kiosk-table. The projection *now* featured a colorful rendering of the irregular galaxy the Ship had just crossed into a few years ago. Icono-telemetry floating about, depicting where the Ship was and the various galaxy in the astronomic cluster.

"Even now," the audible continued as the computerable enlarged the Canis Major system's graphics, "we still have not given proper names to these systems...but to answer your question, Geologist Natsome, there *is* one planet in the Ship's current trajectory, and it has *potential* hospitable conditions for humans!"

There were gasps of hope among those attending the emergency meeting—some even tearing up.

"Mind you, it *is* nearly one year *out* from us at the Ship's current velocity," the audible actuator qualified, but this did not seem to dissuade the humans!

At that point, the colorful projection enlarged even further and depicted a relatively large planet with three small moons orbiting it. "We've utilized the Bayer nomenclature of deep-antiquities, but for *this* planet, and we've designated it as *cMaj*—named after the Canis Major system... conversely, the air is a bit thick for humans—oxygen levels is around twenty-*five* percent and since it's a much bigger terrestrial planet than where humans originated from, the gravity *and* the atmosphere are a lot heavier than you would like—"

"I recommend we *increase* the speed of the terrestrial cylinder to match the gravity of cMaj," Astrophysicist Keyton venBot blurted out; optimism on his countenance—also, he stood straight up from his chair while doing so! "That way our sisters and brothers of the Ship can acclimate to the planet!"

There were applauds upon Astrophysicist venBot's suggestion!

"That is highly recommended, Astrophysicist venBot," the stern actuator of the Ship commented. "I might also recommend we do the same to match the atmospheric makeup of cMaj...are there any objections from the humans attending this meeting?"

Everyone in the conference room looked around and just about every one of them shook their heads; having no objections. The way things were governed on the ancient generational ship was mostly communal. But de facto, the Ship's actuator systems functioned as the leader of that human-communal organization of scientists, engineers, maintenance crew, and the various civilian and military agencies that ran the ancient society on a daily basis.

The generational Ship was not a democracy; nor was it an autocratic system. It simply seemed logical to the humans within that asteroid-sized ship to *let* the computerable system take the lead on, literally, steering the ship of humans that would prove too complicated for them!

"We'll need to come up with a media campaign," Mirandana Ellisante, Tyra's boss, threw out to the group. She directed her attention to a group of professionals seated at a kiosk-table a bit further back...most of them were from the *civilian* agencies that dealt with human health-related subjects and societal issues. "It probably would be nice to have projected mediums *and* personal-public engagements about the upcoming changes to the cylindrical sector of the Ship—so the populace won't be afraid and would have time to adjust."

There were several affirmations from the group, the optimism from the meeting emanating from the civilian professionals as well.

"Do we really need to tell them," Dambudzo, a well-known psychologist, curtly put to the meeting. There was an uncomfortable silence after her question, but she continued. "Trust me, sisters and brothers, in *my* field we have a long history of humanity acting as a river of consciousness that is not necessarily bad; *but* nor is it necessarily *good*! I wonder how an enclosed spaceship of two-and-a-half-million people will behave when they've learned we are *low* on fuel for the very thing that's kept them *and* their civilization alive for an eon!"

Once again, there was a stir in the large meeting.

"Psychologist-Dambudzo," this time it was main tech Tyra Housenn that decided to jump in, "are you suggesting that we wait until the Ship is *closer* to cMaj a little less than a year from now, or that we do not tell the populace at all?"

"I say we never tell them at all!" Again, a stirring among the large group of humans at the various kiosk-tables. The psychologist tried to clarify for them. "Remember some of the more recent political movements we've had with some in society...like the group that tried to convince all of the elderly in the populace to commit euthanasia so they could make *more* room for the younger citizens on the Ship! How many of our elderly had we lost to those avaricious idiots?"

"Hundreds," main tech Housenn responded grimly; given that she was the one to question the psychologist.

Psychologist-Dambudzo gave a terse nod. "Indeed, Maintenance Technician Housenn, many speculate that *some* of those suicides were not suicides at *all*! And, now, we're going to tell those very same people our planet-ship is about to run *out of fuel* in just two decades..."

The psychologist's retort was poignant. Indeed, Tyra was able to see that she was the perfect fit for such profession!

"Psychologist-Dambudzo raises a very important issue," the Ship's actuator audible came back into the meeting. "Shall this gathering inform the greater-populace of the nuclear fuel issue or not?"

It was with this issue that the humans in charge of running the generational Ship truly found complicated! They all looked around their respective kiosk-tables; uncertain how they should respond!

"Perhaps the humans should vote on it—via the raising of hands?" the actuator asked.

The large group of humans, as if demonstrating that river of consciousness that Psychologist-Dambudzo had just addressed, automatically fell in line.

"All *for* informing the populace," the Ship's audible system stated—approximately one-third of the governing humans voted *for* it with upheld hands.

"All for *not* informing the populace..."

This time, the *two-thirds* that did *not* vote with the first group all held up their hands.

A bit of mumbled conversations after the vote, but the actuator went on. "It is official, then...the attendees of this meeting *must* respect the vote of this governing body by its majority. I've recorded the vote—indeed, the whole proceedings—so it is incumbent on *each* member *not* to inform the greater population of this ship's dwindling fuel."

That included maintenance tech Tyra Housenn...whom, in fact, voted *to* inform the public...

CHAPTER THREE

A Time...

The four-star systems within the Canis Major irregular galaxy had been gradually getting brighter—from the perspective of the residents of the generational Ship—for close to a year at that point. Many residents, *at first*, had not noticed the subtle changes in the gravitational-spinning colony, as the centrifugal speed slightly *increased*. Or that the artificial air had become richer—emergency crews all over the colony had noticed a marked increase in bigger fires within buildings and even in a few open-air fields where farming colonists *swore* they made sure to shut down their machinery to ensure nothing caught on fire. Such was due to the scientists within the governing organization pumping in a bit *more* oxygen, so that the Ship's artificial air would gradually match that of planet cMaj.

There, actually, *were* educated and suspicious citizens that *had* noticed. There was a small movement of residents organizing themselves within their local sectors; forming what amounted to monitoring organizations that were counterbalances to the Ship's *official* governing organization! But the actuator system dispatched an army of infiltrators to *all* those groups. The various agents within those local citizen organizations did a good job in tampering down many of the locals' suspicions and monitoring of the Ship's governance.

All that worked perfectly for the Ship's government of its actuator systems and its large groups—or, "nodules"—of human professionals...But then came the news over Maintenance Technician Tyra Housenn's personal media kiosk at her abode, within the immense, spinning colony's residential sector...

The projection's event-alert—as was custom for news of Tyra's generation—was simple: it showed several pictions of various citizens, while in the background a moving piction of the event itself. Iconographics hovered, giving brief but poignant details of the event, and the news-alert was over...

That is to say, the news being the *storming* of the Office of Infrastructure's headquarters by a large mob of residents that had enough of a year's-worth of changes in the colony's ecosystem and being told it was all in their heads!

"My stars," Tyra blurted out to herself in her one-person residence. She looked around her abode; feeling a pit in her stomach after remembering that almost a year ago, the Ship's governing-nodes of its actuator systems and the circles of human professionals had voted to keep the citizens of the Ship in the dark about the Ship's dwindling supply of nuclear energy...and now, as a consequence of that vote nearly a year ago, a large portion of the Ship's citizenry were suspicious of their governing-nodules and were, *now*, pretty much at an official revolutionary stage!

As Tyra quickly dressed herself from a simple domestic gown to a public attire, her own residential actuator inquired, in a female voice to match the resident living within, "Tyra, do you think it is a good idea to go out tonight, with the uprising at Infrastructure's headqu—"

"It's all the reason *more* for me to go, Home-Synth! I've never told anyone else—not even *you*—but I have *some* responsibility, in my own way, of what's happening tonight!"

"I see...then I bid you good fortune, Maintenance Technician Tyra Housenn. I only *hope* I will see you again."

Tyra knew it was the actuator's way of trying to discourage her from going out. And it did not work...

She lived in a section within the Cylinder that was a bit further out from the center of the spinning, circular landscape of open lands and intermittent clusters of towns that were strategically scattered from each other...again, thank the ancestors for having the foresight to design a balanced planet-like ecosystem! But that was all deceptive, really, Tyra could now truly see...

Being a bit farther away also meant Tyra had to contract a vehicle from one of her local township's mass-transit division. For during the artificial night-cycle there weren't a lot of commuting land- nor air-transportation doing their pre-programmed routes. Given she was, obviously, in a hurry, Tech-Housenn ordered a single-flyer that was not much bigger than two adults put together!

She conducted her purchase at the kiosk of the transportation depo of her town, hopped into her leased single-flyer, selected her destination, and the vehicle zipped off into the colony's artificial night sky; joining a traffic of flitting transporters already lighting the night...

CHAPTER FOUR

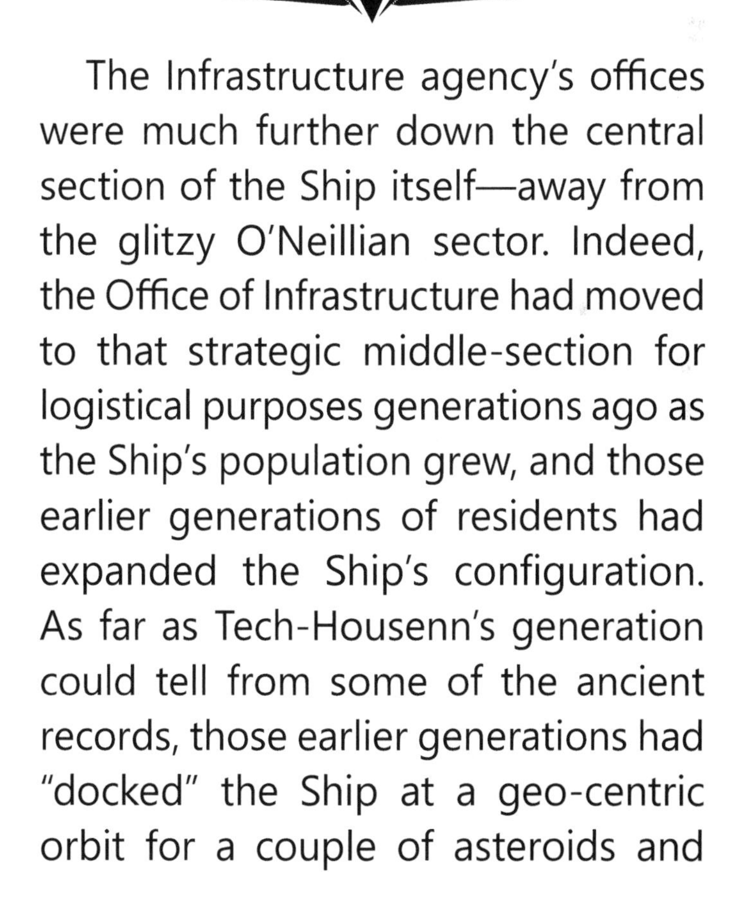

The Infrastructure agency's offices were much further down the central section of the Ship itself—away from the glitzy O'Neillian sector. Indeed, the Office of Infrastructure had moved to that strategic middle-section for logistical purposes generations ago as the Ship's population grew, and those earlier generations of residents had expanded the Ship's configuration. As far as Tech-Housenn's generation could tell from some of the ancient records, those earlier generations had "docked" the Ship at a geo-centric orbit for a couple of asteroids and utilized their elements by mining them for building-materials...

That same Office that had spearheaded such lofty engineering feats those generations ago was *now* under attack by several *thousand* of the Ship's citizens!

Maintenance Tech-Housenn was jostled among the horde of mostly younger people as she plowed her way through the knot! Along with human security, there was a battalion of tall synthetics that were of the specialty design—their specifications being more hardy and intimidating looks to mostly scare off rioting citizenry.

The captain of the enforcement forces recognized Tech-Housenn from previous businesses within the Ship. Standing next to him on the balcony, as they monitored the situation, were three nodule-members—Psychologist-Dambudzo, Shipmate Billamont Harvester, and Astrophysicist-Keyton venBot. Captain Marcus Sommerst got all three's attention and pointed her out to them. They all flinched with surprised gasps at seeing the small, young woman within the boiling crowd as she clearly was having trouble trying to reach them!

The captain spoke into his comm-device and one of the militarized synth's jets fired up and it flew over and then *into* the mob—rioters scattering just before it virtually crash-landed right in front of Tech-Housenn! The synthetic then grabbed Tyra and flew back over to the elevated section of the facility; joining Captain Sommerst and the three nodule-members. The synth stood by, waiting for Captain Sommerst's next orders before it flew off to join the other synthetic enforcers.

"Don't hurt them, Captain," Tyra called out to him over the clamor as more of the towering synthetic beings were ordered by the captain to go out into the crowd and box them in! "They're just frustrated about the living conditions we've imposed on them!"

Nodule members Dambudzo and Harvester both looked upon the young maintenance technician with appraising eyes, then glanced at each other but kept their thoughts to themselves.

"Where are some of the other nodule members," Tyra asked any of the others nearby.

"We advised them to stay away after it started to turn *this* ugly," Astrophysicist-venBot explained. "We didn't expect *you* to come, otherwise we'd have sent you the same message, Tech-Housenn!"

"I was part of that meeting; I feel I should help!"

The scientists gave her a *different* appraising look from that of his colleagues. Respect...

The riot suppression by the synths was successfully walling off the rioters from the Infrastructure's facilities; pushing the crowd down toward a more open area of the Ship's interior.

"Of course, you know what this means," Psychologist-Dambudzo put to the small group; all turning their attention to her. "This will be the start of the latest movement, of a long *list* of movements, of this ship's very long history!"

The three other nodule members and the captain either nodded their heads or quietly absorbed the words of the psychologist.

"Hold them there," Captain Sommerts said to his forces via his hidden comm, "let some of their agitation run its course...if they're as logical as they're portraying themselves to be, they'll think otherwise and disperse without *us* having to take them into custody!"

Tyra could see from their high position on the balcony the seven-foot tall synths gradually form a mechanized wall of enforcers, and on the other side, the thrashing rioters. Some, she noticed, were gesturing to the nodes on the balcony—placing their hands over their throats, as if someone were choking them! An apparent reference to, in fact, the Ship's scientists releasing a higher level of oxygen and other elements into the Ship's artificial air; thinking it would do the populace some good to acclimate them to their up-coming dock with planet cMaj...

Which, by the way, the governing node-government, along with the Ship's actuator system, had *yet* to tell the colonists about...and when they eventually do, they all knew, the *real* trouble with the populace would happen! Psychologist-Dambudzo's words of a new movement were, indeed, poignant...

CHAPTER FIVE

Days had passed since the uprising of thousands of the Ship's citizens at the Office of Infrastructure. Maintenance Technician Housenn had a day off from her official vocational duties, and she was determined to investigate the Ship's situation with its depleting nuclear fuel all on her own! There were some things about the situation with the Ship's history that seemed a bit patchy and Technician Housenn didn't want to chance it to a group of professionals that were not likely to be cooperative with such missing data.

She was among the youngest of the governing nodule-government, from the Maintenance node of that system. So, frankly, she was not taken that seriously among most within that governing body. Tyra saw it. She did a good job of ignoring the looks from the older and/or more educated within the nodules' disciplines, especially during the large meetings the nodule would hold for Ship-businesses. Hence, why she packed her torso-strapped computerable and her personal technical equipment and quietly set out for the enclosed area of the Ship during the colony's night cycle!

As her portable device told her the first time, when she had gone in nearly a year ago, the radiation from whatever incident happened with the nuclear had mitigated to the point of moderate levels. She didn't want to risk even low levels of *any* kind of radiation, but her portable explained to Tyra that the half-life breakdown of the enclosed sector's radiation levels were to the point that she could spend up to two days inside—but no more than that!

Again, before she flew off to the ancient sector of the Ship, Tyra's personal actuator at her home tried convincing Tyra not to go—it was a maternalistic/paternalistic synthetic-programming that her parents had *personally* created for her when she left on her own from their household. They wanted, at the very least, a portion of themselves with her after she had graduated to adult status a couple of years ago and moved out on her own.

One of the advantages in working for the Office of Infrastructure was one had access to maintenance portals that were not meant for the average citizens to go through. Maintenance Tech Housenn utilized her knowledge of that network of maintenance, subterranean portals so that she was able to evade the Ship's security tech-observers and its foot-patrol of synth guards...Technically speaking, Tech-Housenn was not breaking the law, but, rather, *protocols* when she gained access to that ancient enclosure via *another*, much smaller portal that she found.

This time, with no synthetic laborers to help her, she utilized her technician's tools to loosen up and opened the ancient portal—*this* one, about the size of a personal-hatch meant for emergency exiting, she speculated. Tyra made sure to quietly close the tiny hatch behind her so that no one would notice...

With all of her equipment attached on her person, or hooked onto her service-belt, Tyra had her portable engage its flood lights *and* bring up a permanent projection of diagrams of where they were in the one million-plus square feet ancient section. She took some time to examine the projection of the enclosed section of the Ship and decided to go a different route from her first incursion into the darkened and, oddly, clean ruins.

As she made her way through the sectioned-Chamber, Tech-Housenn saw more of those odd characters posted throughout the walls and postings—those Letters, Words, and some type of iconographics of *their* ancient times that reminded Tyra of her generation's system of communication. But a different "dialect" of iconography...what were those odd, geometrical shapes with the Writings for? Some were stark-red. Others, yellow... Green was another color she saw constantly in the ancient posts and signs.

As she was spellbound by the history and archaeological contents of her informal investigation of the Ship's nuclear depletion, Tyra kept finding even *more* historical artifacts and sections within the eon's old chamber that stole her attention from her mission! One was a section that was recessed into the walls of the Chamber and seemed to function as some kind of public teaching facility. For there were large, still images within rectangular frames hanging on the walls of this section—*Paintings*, as she remembered from her history classes. Paintings of people from those ancient times of humanity; when they had *first* taken to other astronomical bodies and began to trek *outside* of what was called *Mother Earth* by some and began to colonize the solar system that was thousands of years *behind* Tyra's generation's Ship...

She stopped to looked at the paintings, specifically of the ancestors. They were of varying ethnic families, but clearly humans hadn't change all that much in all the thousands of years! The clothing and how humans expressed their cultures, of course, *did* change a lot...

"Founders of the Ship," Tech-Housenn speculated to her portable device in the stark silence; a slight echo in the Chamber.

A pause from the portable. "Given the attention to display these portraits in this public forum's space, it would seem so, Tech-Housenn...So much of our Ship's history was lost from so many changes in the Ship's actuator's programming, not even the computerables can even give accurate speculation on many of these ancient, cultural sites!"

The last statement gave Tech-Housenn an idea. "Portable, is it possible for you to catalogue *all* of the characters and iconographs you've seen—from our first trip here a year ago, to today, and *then* try to run some kind of estimate-translation of the Ancients' language?"

There was no pause from the device for that question! "Indeed, Tech-Housenn...I hope you don't mind, but I've already *started* to do that!"

She chuckled with a shake of her head. "I should've known...have any clues at this point what all this is saying?"

"Again, Tech-Housenn, it's just an estimate-translation, but these individuals *were*, indeed, the founding members of the Ship and its colony. Most of them were scientists, at least by their era's standards...Tech-Housenn, I'm afraid there was a *lot* more to the Ship's creation than a mere philosophical destination of humanity. Apparently, there was a catastrophic event at the *solar system level* of humanity's home..."

Tyra froze. She said nothing; letting her portable continue. "If I am interpreting this archaic system of writing correctly, humanity of our founder's generation had some kind of technology that *directly* utilized their home-star...I don't understand it all, Main Tech-Housenn, but the bottom line is, something went horribly wrong, and that system of technology the ancients were using in Mother Earth's star system was so pervasive, it basically *destroyed* humanity!"

"What? I don't understand what you're saying, portable...was it an *accident* with the techno—?"

"—I'm afraid it was a *war,* Tech-Housenn...and, Tyra—this posting on the wall...I'm so sorry, but apparently, *this colony is all that is left of humanity*!"

CHAPTER SIX

Maintenance Technician Tyra Housenn did not care if she were to be reprimanded for her unofficial foray into the Enclosed sector of the Ship, she had her portable contact the *entire* governing nodule, including the Ship's actuator. She did this while they were still inside the enclosed section, just in case there were any questions about the site and Tyra would be able to share on-locale. There was no need to have a physical meeting for what she had to tell them of what she learned about the *true* reason for the Ship's journey, thanks to her portable's translating the dead language of the ancients.

When every single member of the nodule connected—visually and projected-wise, Tyra handed over the entire presentation of their tour of the Enclosed section to her portable. It replayed major parts their investigation, including the last few minutes of the portable's translating the ancients' language. For verification, some of the nodes in the government asked that the Ship's actuator, as a second opinion, also take a look at the portable's recordings of all the ancient texts and iconographic characters.

The actuator verified Tech-Housenn's portable device's translation of the ancient text...

And just as the nodule governance had done nearly a year prior, the Ship's actuator conducted a vote from the human nodes; right there, after Tyra's portable concluded its presentation. There simply was no time to waste to put off the vote for a sit-down that would take weeks to organize, given everyone's schedule! That time, however, the subject of the vote was piled *atop* the issue of the depleting nuclear fuel of the Ship to, now, include informing the *whole colony* of the plans for docking with planet cMaj in the Canis Major system, and finally, the fact that their entire reason for existing was to keep homo sapiens *alive* in the universe!

Now that the governing nodule had voted to inform the total populace of their whole situation as a generational ship, the more public division within the nodule had to get into action. The communications crew within the nodule, at *first*, had to coordinate with the Military division nodes. To make sure the Military and its security sub-division had its people and super-synths in place around the entire Ship, should the terrible revelation of the Ship's fate be received with violence by some of the citizenry. After all, it had only been about a week since the uprising by thousands of citizens outside Infrastructure's headquarters.

Once the Military had its teams and troops in position throughout the Ship—which took a couple of days, only *then* did the human nodules decide to tell the Ship's actuator they were ready for *it* to do a rare all-Ship public notice...

CHAPTER SEVEN

...Times...

"...One week until the Ship reaches planet cMaj...One week until the Ship reaches planet cMaj...One week until the Ship reaches planet cMaj!"

In deep ancient times, in a religion that was called Christianity, the temples called churches would ring large bells that were atop those temples to call for worship service, or to keep track of time. In a similar religion that was not quite as old, Islam, *that* faith's temples had men call out—in towering structures, just like the bells for Christians, when it was time for its adherents to pray...in a strange twist of human fate, eons later, humans, now, had gotten a calling high above, but from a synthetic voice over the spinning, cylindrical colony! Readying the people for their upcoming destiny with a world they knew nothing about... except that it was much bigger than their home-planet and its atmosphere was a bit heavier than what evolution had rigged their lungs to breathe in!

The booming voice, alternating between female and male, was part of the Ship's actuation and was emitted via strategically placed speakers throughout the whole Ship, not just in the O'Neillian sector. Even out in the countryside of the spinning colony, where there were farms with limited animal species and undulating hills and pastures, the Ship's multitude of media-kiosks were tucked away in trees, rocks, and other natural locales.

The announcements were always in threes, and always during the quarter-mornings. Of course, given that the Ship was a high-tech marvel, the announcements weren't *necessary*, given all the communication technologies the Ship and its citizenry had. The idea came from the media division within the nodule-government, utilizing history and psychology—*A shared destination should have shared messaging*, was how Psychologist-Dambudzo put it...

With one week until ETA was reached at cMaj, the swirling-atmosphere-orange planet had already been the biggest *and* the brightest astronomical body in the Colony's sky—that is to say, images beamed that were acres-sized projections that were an echo of the ancient concept of windows; rectangular and depicting whatever local-space setting the generational-ship was traversing at that time. cMaj's three moons were a treat for the colonists to see by themselves—for one of the moons, *alone*, was a world of natural resources that the Colony would be able to utilize *somehow*—to say nothing of the planet itself!

This was a Time of jubilation for the Colonists, despite many citizens *still* suffering from the acclimation adjustments within the Colony. For mere days ago the nodule-government had imparted to them the troubling discovery of how the Ship was running low on its antediluvian fuel of nuclear! And now, an entire world—plus its satellites!—was just within grasp of the Society!

But that period of jubilation was still tempered by the, *also*, recently discovered monument by

Maintenance Technician Tyra Housenn and translated by her portable *and* the Ship's actuator...that, according to the sacred shrine Tech-Housenn and the nodules shared with the rest of the Ship, the Colony *was* the vestige of homo sapiens from a planet called Earth. And to the best of the nodules' understanding, *there were no other generational-ships or colonies besides them*!

Just as Poul Ean, one of the science-nodule members, stated a year ago during that fateful meeting upon the nodules' first time learning of the Ship's nuclear fuel crisis, the Ship's governing body had to draft a scouting mission to cMaj and its three moons. It was not enough to *only* take computerated information. The mission, staffed by the nodule-governing humans from the various scientific disciplines and their supporting crew, would have to physically *go* to the planet and see if it could even remotely support all or most of the Ship's population of two-and-a-half million citizens! Most likely, the mission would have to split up between cMaj and the three lunar bodies...

The scouting mission was assembled by the end of that *last* week upon the Ship's arrival of the cMaj's system!

While the planet-ship's populace—most of it, anyway—had thrown festivals and official commemorations in each township within the spinning sector of the Colony, the nodule-government had been working on getting the nodule-scouts ready for launch to the cMaj system. Heading the entire mission was Astrophysicist Cairo an Preun. He, *did*, in fact, split up the scouting mission so that he would take a slightly bigger team, given cMaj was, obviously, an immense body. The three other, smaller teams would be headed by other astro-scientists of the nodules.

Included in an Preun's crew was Main Tech Tyra Housenn. She was chosen by the nodes, themselves, to work on Astrophysicist-an Preun's team! Tyra had done well in the past year investigating the enclosed chamber of the Ship—especially finding that ancient warning signal about the nuclear fuel levels, and *then* with discovering the Ship's ancestral monument that told the history of Mother Earth's demise, the young technician was duly awarded for her work.

But while in the cabin of the main scouting ship as it was making inroads into cMaj's atmosphere, she was beginning to wonder if she had done a fatal mistake taking on the mission!

"...Stars, we're not even going to see the terrain if we keep shaking like this," Tech-Housenn said over the cerebral-comm as the utilitarian, rectangular scout ship was buffeted by severe turbulence!

"It's just the local storm," Mechanic-Charmain Sohill reassured over the cerebral-comm from his strap-seat. "We're a population that's not used to atmospheric turbulence...in the Cylinder, back on the Ship, it's always a perfect day!"

"Huh!" She felt like she was going to vomit!

The scout ship continued its rattled descent for several more miles before it finally cleared the storm system and the crew was finally able to see the curving, expansive land of cMaj after Pilot-Lanay Thuall retracted the metallic glass-shield protectors.

Everyone in the ship were able to read the scout ship's actuator telemetry on the planet via their respective cerebral-comms, which most had already known for a year, after the governing nodule's meeting on the Ship's fuel problem—dense atmosphere by human-standards; high-carbon dioxide levels; less moister, and that was mainly due to the hotter temperatures on cMaj than, say, the humans' Mother Earth. The only team members that had *not* known anything about cMaj until the Ship's actuator had given a Ship-wide public notice were Pilot-Thuall and Mechanic-Sohill. For neither were node-members of the governing body.

"Fillip, see any signs of vegetation,"

Astrophysicist an Preun asked the geologist.

Everyone else could see that, with their bare eyes, they could *not* see *any* greenery from such heights in their craft. But a geologist was able to distinguish subtle colorations on the terrain that arced the entire horizon before them!

Geologist-Natsome made a hesitant noise before responding. He was looking at the data from the ship's projections and using his skilled eyes. "Don't let these clouds fool you, everyone...lot's of methane in them... there *is* some kind of vegetation, Cairo, but it's probably pretty sparse! But I see *some* promise..." A shrug from the geologist.

The atmospherics were more in Chemist-Luciana Salomenes' expertise area. "Indeed, that's what

I'm understanding from these measurements and just from first impressions, Cairo. All things taken into account, mission commander, we lucked out in finding a planet with *this* meager amount of ecology!"

"Actuator," Astrophysicist-an Preun put to the scout ship's system, "are these readings consistent with the *whole* planet, from what you've scanned so far?"

The scout ship flashed an iconographic animation that was seen in each of the scout member's cerebral-comm; denoting it was the *fourth* scan it had taken of planet cMaj. "With the slightest of variation, but, correct, Astrophysicist-an Preun."

The astro-scientist glanced about the cabin at the other scouting crew. "Looks like we'll have to start civilization from scratch on this planet, everyone...bit disappointing, but it's what we have!"

"I'm not complaining," Maintenance Technician Housenn volunteered with perseverance; still remembering how close their colony came from being marooned in deep-space in twenty-years' time had they *not* taken the opportunity to dock with cMaj!

"What's next in protocols," Chemist-Salomenes asked the scout-leader as she began doing some of her own computerized search on the planet from her seat's console.

"Finding a good landing spot... deploy our synths—I'm thinking something like five hundred miles at a radius from the landing point for each one of them..." an Preun shrugged as he glanced about the spreading landscape before them in their descending ship. "We've got time, *now*...I'd say let the synthetics do their own scouting while we do ours and take it from there."

Again, the mission-lead glanced at his team to gauge their opinion. Everyone else nodded and gestured in consent.

"Actuator," an Preun addressed the ship's system, "could you patch me to the other scout-parties?"

"Done," was the simple response.

Seconds later, the voices of the three other scout-leads—each party for cMaj's three moons, came through; affirming that they were connected. Astrophysicist-an Preun told them of his plan for scouting cMaj's terrain and suggested that each of their, respective, teams should do the same format. For with the nodule-governance, it was not a hard and fast system, so an Preun really did more advising than he did supervising. Nevertheless, the three other scouting leads agreed to the astro-scientist's approach and would contact him should the situation warrant it.

CHAPTER EIGHT

Tech-Housenn *still* found herself mesmerized by the sight of the Colony's generational-ship; so big in the planet's night sky that it appeared as a nearby star; a beacon of stasis as it remained docked at its geo-centric orbit around cMaj. At first, Tyra thought of the mothership as the anchor. But, of course, if the planet's atmosphere were the water and the Ship a boat at sea, what were the scouting missions on cMaj and its three moons, then...?

Suited up in her space-protectant, she was taking a break from setting up the small scouting party's semi-permanent camping grounds. She was used to having synthetic laborers do most of the manual tasks whenever she worked on projects, but the synths the scouting crew had were already traveling toward other regions of the continent they were on. The synths did this via their built-in rockets, but they merely skimmed the ground...they weren't aircraft, so they couldn't go too high. Plus, it was a way for the mechanized beings to preserve their energy.

The five other scouting members were, also, taking a respite. Each one of them doing their own thing to relax. After they all had gone back inside their scouting ship in order to eat a meal, some stayed inside a little longer; others suited back up and took some alone time outside the ship.

--Static came over the cerebral-comm...

It caused the maintenance technician to flinch out of surprise! She looked back at the camping grounds to see if it was any of her crewmates. But, via her cerebral-comm, Tyra was able to tell it was *none* of them.

"Lunar scouting teams One, Two, and Three, this is Maintenance Technician Tyra Housenn...did any of *you*, or your synths, try to contact me?"

Well, that caused her scouting crewmates at the camping grounds to sit up or look out of the scouting ship and put their attention onto Tyra!

"Negative on engaging comm with you or with *any* of your scouting crew, Tech-Housenn," came Astrophysicist-Marrisa Pumont of lunar scouting party number One.

"That's a match, here," came the voice of lead-scout for the lunar search party number Two, Astrophysicist-Benn Latun.

"So," voiced Astrophysicist-Zeene, of lunar scouting party number Three, "you know I'm going to say it was *not* me...what are you saying, Tech-Housenn; you got some kind of interference?"

"Synthetics of cMaj scouting party," came the leader of all of them, Astrophysicist-an Preun, "Scout-Lead inquiring if any of you tried 'comming Maintenance Technician Housenn or anyone else from any of the scouting parties?"

All five of an Preun's synthetics responded, Negative...

...there was silence over the entire, four-party scouting mission's comm-network!

"Probably just some feed from the Colony," one of the scouting members from lunar scouting team number Three speculated over the cerebral-comm.

"Then why don't *any* of us hear static *now,* or from when we first landed on cMaj," Tech-Housenn contested.

No response from her scout-mates...

"Tech-Housenn," Astrophysicist-an Preun said over the comm, "why don't you come back to the camp...this is *not* one of your famous excursions back on the Ship. I don't want to take any chances...Your parents would boil the life out of me if something were to happen to you!...Which of you synthetics on cMaj is closest to our campgrounds? I'd like two of you to re-direct back to the campgrounds..."

"Number *Four,* Astrophysicist-an

Preun," synthetic laborer number Four spoke up over the cerebral-comm.

"Number *One*, here, as well, Astrophysicist-an Preun...we're about the same distance from the camp right now."

"Number Four, please divert your trajectory to the camp...I never thought I'd actually say this on an otherwise-empty planet, but we might need you to guard us! Number One...please continue with your mission. One synth should—"

"If I may, mission commander," synth One rebutted, "but there is a total of *five* synths on this mission under your direct command. Three *other* synths can, yet, cover a great distance...I highly recommend having *two* synthetics at the base with the humans under these conditions."

Astrophysicist-an Preun glanced at

the others on the base for a gauge. They merely shrugged. As did the mission commander.

"That's an affirmative, synth Number One...synths Two, Three, and Five, continue your tasks as given!"

CHAPTER NINE

"Cairo...Cairo..." Geologist-Fillip Natsome, clad in his space-protectant, nudged the astrophysicist a bit harder on his arm. *"Astrophysicist-an Preun*!"

The scouting mission lead snapped out of his sleep in his bunk; aft-section of the scouting ship, where there were personal compartments for tiny private areas for the crew. He looked around the small section and noticed that all the other bunks were vacant. Natsome went on...

"Tech-Housenn and I stayed up all night waiting for synth Number Four to show up..."

The astro-scientist's head snapped up. "It never did?"

The geologist simply shook his head; a deeply worried countenance on his face. And after the astrophysicist learned of the news, there were *two* faces with deeply worried countenances.

"Where's everyone else," an Preun asked as he got up and started to slip his space-protectant back on.

"They're outside, *still* trying to locate Number Four. Synth One had been scanning all night for Number Four—nothing, of course. It's standing guard now. As for *Tyra*; well, you know Tech-Housenn with her wandering ways..."

Again, Astrophysicist-an Preun's head snapped in Geologist-Natsome's direction. "What? I told Tyra to stay on the campgr—"

"You told her, *last night*, to come *back* to the camp. This is *today*, and, frankly, Cairo, that's *why* the scouting mission is here—to investigate, whether or not, the planet and its system is a good place for us to relocate our citizens...besides, she took the mechanic with her."

That seemed to ease an Preun a bit. Whom, by that time, was fully-attired in his space-protectant. Both men exited the parked scout-ship and joined Pilot-Thuall and Chemist-Salomenes at the campground's growing infrastructure of scientific equipment, computerable perimeter fencing, and the four, remaining single-flyer vehicles assigned to the four remaining humans on the campgrounds. Synthetic laborer *One*—the synth that made it back to the base last night—stood ramrod still in the center of the camp; its sensors and comm-systems reading and observing all things in the vicinity...

"...Yes, this time I heard it," Mechanic-Sohill assured Tech-Housenn in a whisper. The two were in an eye-stretching plains region. The hills undulated as if they had been a sea-expanse that had been frozen on the spot, billions of years ago! Their single-flyers were parked several yards away. "Tech-Housenn, how do we know if we're not walking into a trap? These blips of comm-interference...are they just a way to lure us to some *thing's* trap?"

"I can see you don't venture out too often, Charmain...Alright; I've thought about that, too. But we *don't* know. That's *why* the scouting team is here, isn't it? Despite what Astrophysicist-an Preun said to me last night about my excursions, we *have* to take a bit of a risk for our colony, Mechanic-Sohill."

They finished taking readings in that section of the plains—no synthetic laborer Number Four, and nothing to indicate *where* the strange interference came from. Tyra continued after they glanced at their reading from their devices, including their respective portables.

"Look, I've learned not to assume things...last year, after my synths got that portal to the enclosed chamber opened and we had those unexpected readings because of the millennia of trapped air, when news got out about it, some colonists thought *aliens* had been stowaways there and sabotaged *that* part of the Ship just to keep the colonists *away* from there!"

The young mechanic did a sarcastic laugh. "I have a confession to make,

Tech-Housenn...*I* was one of those colonists who *thought* that!"

He could see through her translucent protectant's headpiece that she was smiling and rolling her eyes at his response. The humans were able to breathe cMaj's air, but the light-weight helmets made it easier for them. He saw through that translucent cover that a sudden thought crossed over her.

"Were you *also* one of those that protested the altered living conditions within the Ship during the Acclimation Period? Because the Ship's actuator's stats show they tend to be of the same demographics..."

Maintenance Technician Housenn was beginning to make a name for herself in the media of events within the Colony after her finding of the ancient signal a year ago, so Mechanic-Sohill knew where she was coming from. He gave a thoughtful look at her before responding.

"I'd rather not say one way or the other—"

"—this is synthetic laborer Number Four...Repeat, contacting Colonial Mission cMaj, this is synthetic laborer Number Four..."

Before Tech-Housenn and Mechanic-Sohill could even respond, there was a barrage of responses from the other scout crews; asking where synth Four had been and a few choice words! But Number Four responded, "*You* must evacuate planet cMaj *now*... Repeat, *you* must evacuate planet cMaj *now*...Advised that you do *not* wait for me...evacuate planet cMaj *now*...!"

And synthetic laborer Number Four simply repeated that last message...

CHAPTER TEN

The piloting shipmates of the Colony were taken unaware when the Colonial Mission of cMaj zipped an emergency call to them! For the nodule-government and the Ship's actuator system expected to hear from all four scouting teams as far out as a month. It had only been less than *two* weeks!

All four scouting ships were heading for the mothership at a dead-on collision trajectory as they approached the Colony! And for an unknown reason, there was far too much interference in the Colonial Mission's comm-links to that of the Ship's, so the crewmates and the enforcement nodes could not communicate with the Mission!

The Ship's shipmates had to scramble to their workstations to see if they could guide the Colonial Mission ships in—of course, with each ship's own actuator system, the scout ships needing help flying in should *not* have been an issue *at all* for the Ship's co-pilots! Of course, the super-advanced navigational system of the Ship's actuator network did the actual piloting of the planet-ship. But the *humans* from the nodule-government were *always* the ones in control of the course and actions of the Colony.

Also, the Ship's defenses were having some technical glitches. Supervisors manning control kiosks were giving out orders to the ranks in rooms filled with soldiers and a flood of human and synthetics' communications! Projected moving pictions showed the four scouting ships; some projections showed a myriad of scenes of the Ship with its civilians, outer real estates, and the planet cMaj with its three moons.

The current situation the shipmates and the enforcement nodes found themselves in presented a dire dilemma to them. Should the scouting mission's four ships get too much closer to the generational-ship, Captain Marcus Sommerst would have to make a moral decision between the four scouting teams from the Colonial Mission of cMaj, and the starship of over two million citizens...

The Ship's system had automatically activated its emergency units to the docking area where the four scouting ships had originated from. Both synthetic units *and* human officers were implemented. Captain Sommerst was located elsewhere; within the O'Neillian sector of the Ship. But he was remotely monitoring the situation with his own portable device.

The units' posture seemed more of a defensive stance than that of an emergency task, given their weapons on hand *and* their unit-groups strategically forming one big semi-circle of military and policing machinery! From the Ship's system's *and* the nodule-members' points of view, they didn't know if there had been some coordinated mutiny within the Colonial Mission among its people, or if there had been some technological problem with their ships' actuator—taking over the four scouting ships and was inadvertently aiming them at the mothership at the incorrect speed. At that point, it did not matter to the

Ship's crew. The scouting ships might as well had been missiles!

"cMaj Mission Commander an Preun," the Ship's actuator verbalized over the general comm of the Ship while the enforcement nodule's units were standing at the ready in the dock area, "have your teams reduce their rate of motion *at once...*"

More static...

"cMaj Mission—"

"—peat, this is Mission Commander an Preun, *we are not in the ships! Repeat, we are not in the ships!* Our synths have commandeered them... *shoot on spot!...shoot on spot—*"

There were gasps among some in the human unit!

It was a very rare event, but there were times when the Colony went ship-wide alert over the eon of its *very* long flight: meteor storms, rogue asteroids, precautions of nearby comets...but to *this* generation's knowledge, they didn't recall from history nor of their own experience when it was the *Ship's* very own vehicles that posed the immediate threat to the whole Colony...

...Indeed, its immediate demise!

CHAPTER ELEVEN

...a Half-Life...

cMaj's night sky *still* had that haze; even after twenty years of the Synthetics' Rebellion. No one saw it coming, among the humans. At least, not Tyra Housenn Sohill's generation. It was told of their generation, but as a mere reference: That someday, Humanity would suffer from something called the *Singularity*. Even Tyra's and her husband's teachers and parents weren't exactly sure what that meant, but, apparently, it was that fateful day when the synths had pierced the thick, metallic hide of the old Ship they had landed ashore of planet cMaj.

Tyra's and Charmain's respective portable devices still worked—the advanced technology of utilizing bits of star-energy; bits of molecules floating in cMaj's air...the way the devices understood Singularity, it was a concept that was a tiny percentage of what the average portable inherited from the late-Ship's actuator's systems. Deep in history, Singularity was understood by the computerables to be some tipping-balance. Some reversal of one dominate force tipped over *by* another force. From her days in that once beautiful, spinning planet-like cylinder inside the old Ship, Tyra was told by her grandparents that Singularity was some kind of justice-day! That humans would have to speak up for some of the bad things the species had done to, presumably, *other* species from their ancient home-planet...

Apparently, as Tyra's portable explained to her, Charmain, and the children, there was just enough of the nuclear energy thing in the ancient sector of the old Ship, that when the synths used those scouting ships as missiles, the nuclear inside worked as an explosive-source. Not a lot of the nuclear was left in that old Ship, then. But it was enough to cause the entire Colony to blow—leaving that strange haze in cMaj's sky at nights.

Even some of the Ship's infrastructure survived the blast! Towering, hulks of metal littered parts of cMaj's plains. They were so big, the debris from the old Ship looked like a city that was spread out in the open plains of cMaj! But, of course, much of it was still contaminated by the nuclear. At least, what Tyra's and her husband's portables could scan.

It was ironic. The time of twenty years that had passed since the synths' bombing was the *same* amount of time that the old Colony had left *before* its super-dreadnaught would run out of the nuclear fuel that no official of the old nodule-government even knew was fueling the Ship!

The tiny Housenn Sohill clan consisted of five humans: Tyra, a former technician on the old Ship; her husband, Charmain—former mechanic; the eldest of their children, Miriana (15 years old); Janneca (13); and the youngest and only male offspring, Charl (11).

The other, former Colonial scouting crewmembers of the cMaj planet, *also*, paired up! Their former mission commander and an astrophysicist,

Cairo an Preun, espoused the former chemist of the scout team, Luciana Salomenes. While the pilot of that scouting mission, Lanay Thuall, paired with former geologist Fillip Natsome… those two families, *also*, became their own clans.

It was well understood, that, with the old Colony obliterated, those three clans were, truly, the *last* hope of the species of homo sapiens' viability…for in addition to the defunct generational-ship, the three *other* scouting teams that were assigned to cMaj's three moons eventually died out from natural causes.

There simply was no atmosphere on *any* of the satellites of cMaj. And although those three scouting teams had the technological vehicles and suits to last them for several more years, they simply could not grow produce on barren, lunar surfaces...

For the sake of the cMaj crew that *had* survived, all three of the scouting crews of the three moons decide to cut communications with them. They all knew it would make it easier for the cMaj scouting crew if they did not have to go through the psychological trauma of losing contact with the lunar teams as they died off...

cMaj had a much thicker atmosphere than what humans were used to, true. But it *also* had soil, and moderate rain that had traces of H2o mixed in—just enough for the Three Clans to siphon water with their high-tech, single-flyers and other equipment they *still* had. Plus, they were able to utilize the stored food and seeds they took with them during the scouting mission those twenty years earlier.

Back then, when the old Colony was still alive, it was standard practice for *every* scouting mission to carry produce seeds and extra food. For, as the philosophy went back then: One never knew when the opportunity to seed a new world would come up!

Indeed, there *was* an opportunity for *another* group of survivors of the fall of the generation-Ship: many of the synthetic laborers that were assigned to all *four* of the scouting teams all those years ago!

They were the synths that stayed behind on cMaj and the three moons during the Synthetics' Rebellion on the old Ship. Obviously, since they were synthetic beings, they required no food, no air, and a great deal many other things that humans needed! It was all part of the mutinous synths' plan: wait out the humans as they set up camp on cMaj's three-moon system, while the horde of synths in the Colony would start shutting down many of the old Ship's defenses.

It worked. That vague Singularity balance that so many generations of humans had heard of was finally reached twenty years ago...though, like the humans, virtually all the synth population was wiped out in the Ship's explosion, they *still* had the majority populace within the cMaj system! Not by much, though. Indeed, as the Three Clans families began to slowly repopulate their homo sapiens species, their supremacy by numbers would *not* last long. For they were synthetic beings—they did not have the *ability* to procreate.

Eventually, the surviving synths on planet cMaj took up residency within those *thousands* of building-sized debris scattered on the plains from the destroyed generational-Ship. The radiation levels from the nuclear explosion years prior were manageable, though even the mighty synthetic beings had to venture away from the debris from time to time—just to mitigate their radiation exposure...

Even *before* the remnant-human population on cMaj had become clans, the scouting crew, under Mission Commander an Preun, had escaped with their equipment stashed aboard their single-flyers and managed to find hide-outs in caverns of cMaj's hinter cliffs.

How strange, Maintenance Technician Tyra Housenn, back then, thought to herself as the tiny survivor-populace of humans took to building their permanent camps in the cliffs. She loved history, and she remembered something from her formative school years about homo sapiens dwelling in caves back on their home-planet. For shelter *and* for protection from predators...

CHAPTER TWELVE

"...why can't I go out there...dad said *you* used to go off on expeditions in the old Ship to much worse places when you weren't much older than what I am *now*?"

"Miriana, darling, *we* didn't have rogue synths roaming around back then, either! No, I'm sorry, Miri...one of them could detect your presence there, and then what? Besides, think of all that radiation the debris *still* has from the Colony's blast!"

Tyra Housenn Sohill and the eldest of her children, Miriana, were out scouting for possible regions for the Three Clans of the remnants of humanity to expand into on planet cMaj.

"Mom, all I'm saying is, it would save the Clans a lot of time if we use the debris for a new settlement like the synths instead of starting from scratch...I don't even think they're really interested in fighting us like they used to!"

"Well, things *have* been eerily quiet lately," Tyra admitted, despite herself. "Still...at the very least, even if the Clan Council decided to do what you're suggesting, young lady, it would have to be some of the clutter the farthest out *from* the main cluster...we can't let our guards down, Miri!"

"Affirmed!"

Now mother and elder daughter were gingerly climbing and maneuvering their way through one of cMaj's sharp-edged ridges and inclines of the planet's myriad of cliffs, bluffs, and caves. Strapped to young-Miriana was that old, but reliable, computerated portable device that Tyra used to carry around with *her* during the Old Days...when that spectacular, spinning Colony had an ancient civilization called Humanity. Now, during the post-Colonial era, the near-antique device was Miriana's inheritance from the woman who had found an ancient signal deep in the very foundation of the old Ship. Miriana *also* seemed to have inherited her mother's proclivity for adventuring!

"Well, who does she remind you of, Tech-Housenn," the portable, attached onto one of the teenager's arms, said light-heartedly.

The middle-aged woman chuckled as she found a leveled area of the incline and sat down to rest. Her daughter joined her. They both set their bundle of supplies and equipment down and looked out at the stretching landscape of cMaj, the planet's constant wind blowing their matted hair and their clothes.

"Why does he still call you that," Miriana asked; her eyes surveying the flat and ragged plateau stretching the horizon from their vantage point.

Tyra jutted her head in the direction of the girl's arm. "Why don't you ask him?"

"Your mother will *always* be that curious, scrappy technician to me," the portable said, beating Miriana to the punch. "She had done a lot for the citizens of the Colony in her youth... besides finding that warning signal in the original section of the old Ship—which put us on the path to landing on cMaj in the *first place*—your mother was the youngest member of that governing body we talked about before."

"The notch governance," Miriana tried; her face squinting.

Her mother laughed hardily. It was something she had started doing after the death of the Colony relatively recently.

"The *nodule*-government," the portable corrected. Even though it was a mechanical, the portable seemed to grow wistful at that point. "To be honest with both of you, ladies, I've always thought that Tech-Housenn would take a leading position within the nodule someday...Well, I guess, in a matter of speaking, you *have*, Tyra..."

Now the trio had gone quiet. But not the constant breeze that cMaj tend to have, given its open plains and stretching plateaus.

"*My* turn to present an idea," she quipped with her daughter. Tyra's head jutted toward that stretching landscape. "Portable...what do you think is out there? I was talking with Lanay last week about how the Clans should probably start thinking about spreading out even *more* than we've been talking about..."

Miriana looked at her mother with surprised eyes. Tyra nodded and continued with a shrug.

"All three Clans seem to have adjusted our mini-agricultural schemes to a science; Luciana is pregnant again, I'm sure everyone's heard by now; the oldest of our Clans are still young enough to handle a long trek... Lanay and I think *now* is the time for the Clans to move out while we can! Before Luciana's baby is born. *And* before cMaj's next autumn season...

That's what I plan to put to a vote before the Council."

Tyra noticed the silent spot from her daughter and even the device.

"Too ambitious," she asked them.

The portable was pretty good about letting the humans respond first. So young Miriana spoke up.

"No, no it's actually a good idea, mom...well, you said it yourself: all three families pretty much have gotten our livelihood down to a science—*literally,* right *here*! And from the science that Cairo, Luciana, and Fillip taught all of us since I was a little kid, I'm a little afraid of the unpredictable, mom...it's not like we have a backup if things don't work out, out *there*. I don't know, mom. Sometimes I think you *still* have that culture deep in you that there's some giant colony that's around somewhere that we can call on if things don't turn out the way we think they should."

Tyra seemed to genuinely listen to her daughter. The former maintenance technician silently nodded to Miriana's point.

"Portable...?" Tyra's eyes shifted to the device strapped around her daughter's arm.

"Honestly, ladies, I can see it both ways. In fact, Tech-Housenn, I would even go *further* from the premise you've given. Besides a gradually growing human population and being more secured in your agricultural mini-system you've developed in the cliffs, Tyra, I've noticed something about the synthetics on cMaj in more recent months...their communications with the synths on the *three moons* have increased."

Tyra and Miriana froze.

"You can *hear* their signals," Miriana asked.

"No, of course not...given they are our enemies on this planet, they've made sure to switch to, or created, some new comm-signal that I could *not* interpret. Mind you, I'm able to *intercept* the signals, just not read them. Believe me, I've tried over the years since the fall of the Colony! Miriana, I'm able to pick up interference from them whenever they do long-distant communications..."

"And that could only be the lunar synths they're contacting," Tyra said, nodding to herself.

"Indeed," the portable continued, "and that is why I can see *your* line of reasoning, Tyra, about the Three Clans venturing farther *from* the original campsite on cMaj...I'm only speculating here, ladies, but I'm afraid that the synthetics *may* have an expansion plan of *their* own!"

"That," Tyra speculated, "or the lunar synthetics maybe trying to come *here*, on the planet, and join forces with the other synths!"

Now the two humans looked at one another with fear! Then the adolescent had a thought.

"But I thought Cairo said the synths were limited on how *far* they can fly? So, the lunar synths should *not* be able to come here...I'm sure they would've done it years ago, if they could."

"Oh, the astrophysicist is right, Miriana," the portable said. "As are *you*...They could no more fly to the atmosphere with their built-in rockets than a human could *jump* to it! The Colonists' engineers designed the synths' rockets *only* for augmentation... but *why* else would the synths on cMaj increase their communiques with those on the three moons, if not for consolidating their numbers as the human population grows?"

It was a question that left the two humans in a silent gaze.

CHAPTER THIRTEEN

Tyra and Miriana wasted no time when they arrived back at their home-camping grounds, within the caverns of cMaj's cliffs. Deciding *not* to wait for the Three Clans-vote, Tyra and Mirana, along with Miriana's portable, relayed the conversations they had about the Three Clans' possible need to relocate even farther out from the original campsite. The news about Miriana's portable detecting long-range communications among the lunar synths and the local ones was also brought up. To backup its hypothesis, the portable projected diagrams and pictographic data showing, indeed, the sharp increase of communication among *all* the surviving synthetics!

To avoid the synths' detection on cMaj, all three Clans *always* communicated in person or in pictographic writings, even though their modern communications—such as the cerebral-comms and other communicative devices—were *still* active *and* usable, thanks to the old Colony's usage of photovoltaic tech! The operation of the portable devices among the clans appeared to be safe, they had noticed. The best they could guess, the computerables were self-*contained*, functioning devices. So long as the portables (from each, six adults from the old Colony) did *not* do distant-communications, the entire camps weren't at risk of detection.

Tyra got the idea to Write out the Clans' communications from all those years ago when she and her synthetic laborer technicians had stumbled across archaic systems of Writing. Back then, she had taken it upon herself to learn some of those ancient, and in some cases, dead languages.

Only a few *other* citizens of the old Ship had the knowledge of Writings when the Colony was still alive. Now that Tyra was the only one left *with* that ancient knowledge, she was even more determined to pass on that eon of cultures to her children...

But, of course, it was more than her long love for archaeology and culture. For the most practical reasons, the *very* nascent renaissance of Humanity did not want to risk being detected by the synths. So, the voting would be tricky.

Charmain suggested that all three of the families meet *that* night—at a centrally-located hide-away. That way the trip wasn't too far for any of the families. For, if it was true what Miriana's portable had detected and speculated on about the synthetic beings, the Three Clans needed to make a decision. Preferably, the same night of the vote. Whether or not to take on Tyra's idea of permanently striking out much farther as not only three clans, but as *one Tribe*, at that point...

In the traditions of that old, defunct colony from a far-off star, the humans from the clans randomly picked one of the six portables—one for each, original Colonial member from the old Ship—to chair the voting session. It happened to be Fillip Natsome's device. Like all the other portable devices that survive the bombing of the old Colony from the Synthetics'

Rebellion, Fillip's portable had some wear, even with its voice actuator, but it was in pretty good shape otherwise.

The Clan Council was loosely based on the nodule-governance model from the old Colony. The humans were the voting body, and that included all the adolescent members of the three clans—the children. (Ten years old was the voting threshold, at the suggestion Luciana years prior.) However, the portables could interject, record, and facilitate the convening vote-count...a relatively complex system to govern the tiny speck of Humanity!

It was official: The Three Clans would venture off to cMaj's expansive, plateau-filled horizon and seek to settle that region of the planet! Three of the family-members—Miriana, Bejonan—of Cairo an Preun and Luciana Salomenes, and Filleppe—of

Fillip Natsome and Lanay Thuall, had voted to *not* strike outward; toward the horizon.

But of another subset vote-count—whether or not to lay claim to some of the outer edges of the old Ship's debris field *and* to begin a new settlement *there*...of course, that also meant the strong possibility that the Tribe would then have to take up arms against attacks from the relatively nearby synthetic beings, *plus* some degree of exposure to traces of nuclear radiation from that blast of the old Ship...

Miriana was the *only* person to vote for such idea within the three clans.

Tyra gave her elder daughter a sympathetic look from across the cave after the last vote, all taken within a tucked-away cave in one of cMaj's higher grounds. Miriana simply shrugged with a defeated look. Miriana was genuinely *scared* of that same future...in *that* she was not like her mother—the venturer and former technician that discovered a ticking time bomb of energy for the old Colony. Miriana liked to break out of whatever bubbles that life tended to encase humans in, *but* she liked certainty more.

After the votes and the official closing of the business, as was human nature in group dynamics, the clan members broke into informal sub-gatherings; talking about and reviewing the many serious issues awaiting the small human civilization. As the others discussed and chatted amongst themselves, Tyra saw Miriana quietly leave the cave. She followed her.

Tyra was relieved to see that her daughter only went a few feet from the entry of the cave. She was seated atop a jutting slab of stone.

"You know it's nothing personal," Tyra explained, after sitting next to her and had given her a hug. "They all just don't see any other way to survive so close to the synths. Especially with us slowly growing."

Miriana only silently nodded in reply. But then Tyra noticed how she froze with her mouth gaped! She was looking off to her left, where the cliff had wide ledges, which enabled the humans to traverse the cliffs so well.

That, of course, made her mother shoot up from the slab and started looking from across that ledge of the cliff to see what had shocked Miriana.

It was a sole synthetic being, perhaps about a hundred yards away. Even from that distance, both women could see the synth wore tattered clothing one would typically see on the humans! Even more surprising, the synthetic did something Tyra Housenn had not seen since the old Colony was alive just over twenty years ago—it flashed a short series of lights from its thoracic segment. It was an alternative to high-comm, where there were risks of the synths on cMaj being able to detect such signal. The combination the lights conveyed translated into, *I come in peace. I am synthetic laborer Number Four...*

CHAPTER FOURTEEN

It did not take long for the adolescent children of the clans to take to synthetic Number Four, after they saw how all the parents of the families received him. For long before *they* were born, it was synthetic *Number Four* that had discovered what the other synths on cMaj and its three moons were planning and warned the humans scouting the planet to leave immediately in their ships...of course, the agility and speed of the synthetic beings on the scouting mission at that time overpowered the humans on cMaj and the moons and used the four scout ships as missiles against the doomed generation-Ship...

"...so all this time, you've been out in the plateaus and cliffs," Charmain, the former mechanic from the old Colony, had asked the synthetic. The Three Clans had previously just finished their Council meeting. Now they found themselves in *another* one with their long-lost friend!

"I have, Mechanic-Sohill...I did not want to risk being detected by the other synths so soon after the Rebellion. And, frankly, I wasn't sure how you, humans, would feel having *me* around after my fellow synths had just pretty much obliterated the last colony of your species!"

There were uncomfortable looks traded among the humans after that comment.

"So, why come to us *now*, Number

Four," Lanay, the former pilot asked; her family, the smallest of all the Clans, grouped together at a corner of the cave.

The synthetic actually paused here. A rather human-like trait. Its actuated voice had a slight elctro-raspiness about it. Most likely due to exposure to cMaj's elements in over twenty years! "Colonists, I *am* a synthetic being. Depending where I was on cMaj, I was able to listen in on some of the rogue synthetics' communications with each other and even between them and those on the moons...were any of your portables able to detect an increase of communique between the lunar synths and those on cMaj?"

Most of the humans were already nodding their heads at Number Four's question. But it was Miriana's portable that responded.

"Indeed, Number Four. I had a conversation not too long ago with Tech-Housenn and one of her daughters about it."

The five other portables of the Clans all voiced agreement at Miriana's portable's statement. It continued.

"Apparently, since none of us computerables, *here*, are of synthetic being-status, *none* of us were able to interpret any of their signals—high-comm or otherwise!"

"Old fashioned method called encryption," synth Number Four said. "They, obviously, knew all the humans' portables survived, *and* that the humans had other equipment that could eavesdrop on them. The rogue synthetics simply created an entirely new frequency *and* language that I've just recently been able to crack—mostly...Colonists, I believe the synthetics *have been* in the process of *re-building* portions of the Ship with some of the crash-debris on the planet!"

"—what?"

"—Stars' gravity; no wonder it's been so quiet lately!"

"—if they *all* want to leave the planet, I say *let them go*!"

"—How can they do that with irradiated debris?"

"But they've already started," Number Four insisted, almost having the emotion of annoyance at how the humans seemed to have missed his point. With its almost-natural, angular-structured head—a stylized version of that of a human's—Number Four looked around at everyone in the cave. "I don't know how they're doing it, given the industrial-grade of tools needed...obviously some *smaller* version of the Ship—"

"—would make sense; shorter time; portion-controlled for their numbers!"

"—they're already programmed as walking factories; they'll get it done in just a few years!"

"—but how would they get it off the planet," came the young voice of Lannel, the eight-year old son of Fillip Natsome and Lanay Thuall. His poignant question quieted the cave as everyone thought on it, even the computerables!

"You don't," came the response from Tyra. She got up from her seat of a slab of rock in the cave and began to pace as she thought to herself; the others looking on. "I'm not an engineer, but even *I* know it almost takes ten million pounds of force just to break the escape velocity of most planets! Not even the synths have access to that *kind* of technology on cMaj...No, sisters and brothers and computerables...I think our friends have something *else* in mind!"

"—What does *that* have to do with the increase in their comms?"

"—Maybe they're simply using the debris as scrap for consolidated shelter?"

"—A monument of some kind? Do synthetics do that sort of thing?"

"—A weapon?"

"—Over-kill for such a small population as ours."

"—but what if it's *not* for *us*," Tyra asked bluntly. She looked around at the shocked expressions on the human faces within the cave.

"My love," her husband, Charmain, put to her in a cautious tone, "what are you saying? That there are *more* Colony survivors from the Rebellion—"

"Alien..." came synthetic Number Four's raspy, actuated voice. "Or, to put more accurately, *Domestics*..."

Now every human had gone silent and either had a surprised look on their faces or absolute terror!

"But..." Alexan, eleven-year old son of Cairo an Preun and Luciana Salomenes, spoke up to the whole Council. "We've been here longer than I've been alive! Wouldn't we have spotted them or their prints by now?"

"*Prints*?" Miriana came in. "I don't think something as advanced as the synthetic beings would have to build a super-weapon against some roaming land animals!"

"Indeed. Also, if the domestic society is advanced enough," the portable of Fillip Natsome responded. "If this speculation is true, an advanced civilization *can* remain undetected by visiting aliens—remember, that would be *us*, Council! I think young-Alexan brought up a very good point: It's been *over* twenty years now and none of us have even hinted at detecting Domestics on cMaj. I see no proof of this alien hypothesis."

"Let's test it then..."

Everyone in the cave shifted toward Janneca; thirteen-year old daughter of Tyra Housenn and Charmain Sohill.

"Isn't that what our three scientists in the Clans have taught us all these years...well, *now* that we have this strong hypothesis of *us* being the aliens, we should find out! I would even say, we *need* to..."

The young woman shrugged as she looked around at the other humans with their strapped-on portables and the only synthetic being among them.

CHAPTER FIFTEEN

Tyra indicated that she was in position with the universal hand-gesture of the upward, flicking-motion of one of her palms. Synthetic laborer Number Four replied with the lowest luminosity of lights that could be considered a synth's version of the same gesture.

It had only been a couple of days before when the Three Clans Council held two meetings—the second one, at night and unexpected, was when Number Four surprised everyone and showed up at the miniscule human colony hideout. As a result of that second meeting, the Clans did one more, quick vote. And that sent Tyra and the friendly synth on the mission they were on at that time...just as Tyra's younger daughter suggested during the night meeting: *testing* to see if the synths in cMaj's debris field from the old Ship were building a great weapon, *or* were they constructing some vehicle that could transport them anywhere on the planet, *or,* less likely, were the synths having to deal with *another,* more formidable domestic enemy on the planet?

The duo team was on the very outskirts of the debris swathing junkyard that spanned several miles. There were other concentrations of large debris from the old Ship—after all, the late-Colony's generational-Ship *was* about twenty miles at length, and the synthetics' bombing of *it* was directly above the then-scouting mission. Hence, the biggest share of the Ship's debris was pulled down from its geo-centric orbit by the planet's gravity to the current geography on cMaj. Technically, making it the crash-site for that once-great human colony...

Half-life decay or not, before going on the mission Tyra utilized as much metal scraps she could find around the human settlements within the cliffs of cMaj! Leaving behind her typical produce-grown clothware for around the cliffs, she lined the inside of her space-protectant suit with the scraps and headed off in her, as of yet-working, personal-flyer. Though, despite the hardy-tech of solarvoltaic, *all* the personal-flyers were constantly in need of repairs.

She watched synthetic Number Four from her hiding position among some tangled conduit pipes on the edge of the debris field. That is, pipes around a hundred feet in diameter themselves! Some of the craters formed within the crash site were helpful as well.

Tyra's main job was to *record* the events with a multi-purpose device. The Colonists learned many years ago *not* to zip any comms to each other, given the synthetics on cMaj would be on them in a matter of minutes! Tyra decided not to bring her old portable that she had gifted to her eldest offspring. Should something go wrong, everyone from the Clans agreed it was always important to keep all portables as much as possible. Far beyond Settlement members themselves, the computerables stored virtually an infinite amount of data that helped the tiny human colony survive.

There was one other, uncomfortable

reason for Tyra to accompany Number Four on the mission: There *still* were many of the Colonists who did not want to *fully* entrust a synthetic being on a mission on behalf of the humans. It was an issue that even Four alluded to, but it was as sentiment that Tyra, her whole family, and a couple of others did *not* share. Nevertheless, Tyra agreed to the terms from those Colonists who wanted a *human* to keep an eye on synth Number Four.

She trained the device as it recorded onto synthetic Number Four as he took a fairly-large debris and used his augmented limb to *throw* the piece of metal, literally, almost a mile away—toward the major clumping of the old Ship's wreckage! Number Four immediately ducked back into his cover and watched for whatever results his actions might bring...

Approximately three minutes had gone by before he and the human could see, with their respective devices, a small grouping of synthetic beings converge in the general area where the debris had landed. The synths had, not surprisingly, used their built-in jets to arrive at the scene. They landed on the ground once they'd gotten to the spot—probably to conserve energy.

Tyra silently watched through her device as it recorded the three synthetic beings looking about—with almost a bewildered look that was associated with humans! While all this was going on, Number Four was not just recording via his built-in actuator systems but listening in on their encrypted comms.

Synthetic laborer Number Four had no plans to throw any other debris as bait. The team knew they were already playing an extremely dangerous game to begin with. Most important, Tyra and Four did not want to put the Clans at risk if the duo made too much of a ruckus and the highly intelligent synthetic beings would put the pieces together and conducted a search party for the last of the humans!

After about fifteen minutes, the small grouping of synthetics left that region of the debris field and went back to whatever it was they were doing.

Taking precautions, the duo waited for another ten minutes before they left the crash site; recordings of the events safely embedded in their own devices.

CHAPTER SIXTEEN

"...Alright, we can talk out here," Cairo an Preun whispered after he and former mechanic Charmain led his wife, Tyra, and synthetic Number Four to an area just outside the mouth of the cave that all three of the family clans were sleeping inside at the time. The Three Clans still had not returned to their respective cliff-dwellings since the two meetings. The Clans figured they would wait to see what the results were from Tyra and Four's scouting mission would turn up. Again, living within the reality of not using *any* level of comms so they would not be detected by the synths in the old Ship crash site.

It had been a day since the scouting team of two did their reconnaissance at the debris field of the old Ship. It was well into the night, and this time around, Charmain and Cairo let the families sleep! Tyra and Four were merely giving first impressions of their mission out from the crash site...

"...seems like we agreed to put *both* of your lives at risk for not a lot of information," Cairo stated, slapping a shoulder of the synthetic being. It was one of the few human gestures anyone had seen done to any synth, at least since the bombing.

"Well," Tyra said, standing next to Charmain, "it's not like we presented a real threat to them to get their attention..." She turned her attention to the synth. Since they could not use their comms while skimming back to the camps, Tyra knew no more than anyone else. "So, you couldn't get *any* significant dialogue from them, or *any* kind of background communications going on?"

"Well, Tech-Housenn, it's like you said a few seconds ago: perhaps a more real-world test would've revealed more about what they've been up to. But in order for us to do that—"

"—we'd have to go in deeper into the debris field," Tyra finished; partially exhausted from the mission; partially tired of not finding the answers she'd like to know about their enemies across the vast plains of cMaj. Then she had a thought. "There is *one* thing I've noticed: they seemed...jittered."

The synth's head swiveled between all three humans. "I'm sorry, but there are *still* some human colloquialisms I don't understand!"

"Jumpy," Charmain tried helping; one of his hands gesticulating. "Uh, a bit on the paranoid side..." His own words got him thinking. "Now what, in stars' gravity, would make a gathering of *synthetic beings* nervous?"

All had gone quiet with thought. The strong breeze whipped the men's long, braided hair around. Tyra still had hers bounded up from the mission.

"A boss," Cairo finally said. "Think about it...something unexpected is heard somewhere—"

"—a supervisor sends a small crew to check it out," Tyra input.

"—they find nothing and are nervous about it...?" Charmain said.

"...because they've been attacked *before*!" This was the synthetic that joined the speculation. "Of course...

why else would they communicate with their brethren on the three moons but to *warn* them? By the way, everyone, remember that there were only *five* of us synths on cMaj...with me, here, with *you* that leaves only three rogue synths still on the planet. The other missing synthetic was Number *One*—the one who commandeered your scouting ship for the bombing..."

It appeared that the humans *had* forgotten such details. Understandable; for they had a lot of things on their minds the past several years! They all simply nodded upon Number Four's reminding. He continued.

"Colonists, remember when I said to you the first day I came across your settlement that I've *mostly* cracked their code?"

They all silently nodded. Four continued.

"I believe I can correct you, Mission Commander an Preun, about not getting a lot of information from *this* mission...Months before, when I *first* was able to understand most of the cMaj synthetics' cryptions, they kept making some sort of reference that's never made sense to me: Tardigrades...?"

The synthetic paused, to see if any of the humans had an idea what he was talking about. And, indeed, the astrophysicist did!

"Stars, I thought those were just fairytales from the ancients!"

Tyra and Charmain glanced at each other; lost in the conversation while the synthetic looked on. The astro-scientist obliged.

"Well, I am a bit older than all the other adults in the Settlement, so maybe that's why I've heard of them...Basically, it's part-history, part-children's story, part-poetry that originated from our ancestral planet's moon. I don't know the details, but it's believed these microscopic, Earthen beings—the Tardigrades—accidentally ended up on Mother Earth's moon! Probably during the earliest days of humans venturing out into the oceans of Space...

"Generations later, they kind of became the moon's major pests by the time our ancestors colonized Earth's moon! I guess some families started a tradition of scaring the kids—to make sure they cleaned up after themselves. What do you expect? It *was* the Days of Space-Antiquities!"

A little chuckle from the two other humans. Cairo went on.

"The fairytale-poem went something like...

"We swam the black seas from the graying blue ball, and now we are the king of all!

"We've conquered the Sun and even all its children; we've even captured its essence!

"We've destinied our rights; we've conquered with lights.

"But of all our achievements and of all our mastery, we've been conquered by the tiny—Tardigrades!"

For Cairo, it was a bit of inane nostalgia. He chuckled to himself. He noticed how Tyra and Charmain looked off in cMaj's night; pensively thinking on the fairytale. Synthetic laborer Number Four remained silent. And for good reasons.

"Mission Commander," Number Four said; finally breaking the silence among the four, "now that you've supplied me with a frame of reference for this word, I was able to access historical data on it. *Ancient* data...Sir, did you know that these Tardigrades' biology is so robust, individual-Tardigrades are able to survive in the *vacuum of space*! Provided they're prepared in the right conditions..."

Cairo's smile had been replaced with a concerned countenance. For he knew where the synth was going with his revelation.

"What is more," Number Four continued, "apparently, they are *also* able to survive radiation exposure..."

Epiphany...

The three humans froze on spot; looking at each other, but each one running their own thought-process of the night's impromptu meeting!

"Several generations of the old Ship never really had to deal with them," Tyra said; her eyes looking out at cMaj's night. "Probably a millennial since the Colony pretty much got a handle on other Earthen species—kept the ones we desired, for farming and pets; weeded out those we deemed vermin...except—"

"—except in the *original* sector of the old Ship," Charmain came in. His body language showed he understood the connection! "Where you and your search party years ago discovered that old warning signal...obviously, there was left-over radiation. But whatever Tardigrades that freeloaded *with* our ancestors when they first built the Ship had survived as an organism! And like Four's research backs up, apparently *that* species has *survived* the Ship's bombing from twenty years ago!"

Cairo and Tyra looked at him with dubious eyes.

"Well, why not," Charmain defended.

"Synth Four just said it based on scientific data. Look, if the Tardigrades can survive in *outer space*, what makes you think they couldn't live through an explosion?—as an *organism*, I mean..."

"Stars..." was all that Tyra could say at that point. She began to pace while the two men stood in place; doing a little thinking themselves. Synthetic laborer Number Four kept his silence.

"Have any of you humans wondered *why* the cMaj synthetics seemed so preoccupied with such a micro-organism as the Tardigrade?" Number Four looked at all three of them. They all knew he was being rhetorical. They simply waited for his response. "I don't know about you, Colonists, but I think one of *you* was right to speculate that it's not likely the synths would devote such efforts to build a weapon from the heaps of the old Ship just to fend off simple land animals..."

All three humans' heads whipped around in Number Four's direction!

"What are you thinking, Four," Tyra asked.

"Well, I don't have any proof...I'm thinking of the fairytale by the mission commander. I get the impression, from *it*, that your ancestors saw the Tardigrades more as a *nuisance*-species...if the species were seen as threatening, do you really think your ancestors would've made a fairytale poem about them?

"I'm thinking, An already-rugged organism able to withstand just about every element humans can think of... what's left of the human colony's Ship *still* has some radiation from the nuclear it had originally started off with. Some group of species can undergo changes after two decades under the *right* stimuli..."

Now all three humans converged on synthetic Number Four's spot!

"What aren't you telling us, Four," Cairo asked; a hand on one of the synthetic being's forearms. The two other humans had the same question as the former mission-lead of the original scouting mission. Only, on their faces.

"Don't worry," Four said after a pause, "what I'm about to show you was *recorded* from the scouting Tech-Housenn and I did over a day ago. It's *not* being transmitted..."

All three humans stood back, so they could see the projected recording the synthetic being had done on their mission. Hovering between all four humanoids, the live-recording showed bits of the time Number Four and Tyra were sneaking around on the outer edges of the old Ship's debris field... Number for advanced the recording so that it showed the hiding spot where Four had chosen before he threw a piece of debris a mile toward the major clumping of the debris field...

...Four paused the recording that showed a myriad of severely-clawed footprints all over the ground!

All four humans gasped upon seeing the footprints!

Charmain placed a hand on one of Cairo's shoulders. "Looks like Alexan was on to something the other day!" Referring to the last Clan Council meeting when synth Number Four had showed up that night. For it was Cairo and Luciana's youngest child that made a point about not finding footprints.

"Indeed," Number Four agreed. He,

then, brought up a second projection from his contained actuator files. It was of several moving images of the Tardigrades' various species from several generations gone by. He enlarged one of the images that focused on the feet of the organism.

"Note how the clawed feet perfectly match the prints I recorded over a day ago from the old Ship's debris field." Indeed, the claws on the moving projection showed what could pass as long, curving daggers!

"Gods!" Cairo was repulsed by the eight-legged creature, with its segmented, elongated puffy body and a head the seemingly lacked a face—but for a tubular structure that most likely was its mouth!

"Charmain...Cairo," Tyra said as she took a step closer to Number Four's projections. "The *scale* of these footprints..." She cast a look at synthetic laborer Number Four's face.

"Yes," he responded, "I was hoping you'd all noticed that. Colonists, according to this recording I did of the Tardigrades' footprints, this *current* generation of this species is multiple-times *larger* than that of their ancestors!"

"If I'm using the right scale," Charmain said; leaning in to look at Four's projections better, "each one would be about the size of a new-born feline!"

"Now imagine *thousands* of *those* crawling all over your Clans' caves," the synthetic being said, with almost as much disdain as a human being!

All three humans were, now, shivering in disgust!

"Stars, *this* is why it's been so quiet between us *and* the cMaj synthetics, isn't it," Tyra asked. She kept her eyes on both projections. "I never thought I'd hear myself say this since the Synthetics' Rebellion, but all those poor synths are battling *hordes* of these—aliens!"

"Oh, but they *aren't* aliens, Madam," synth Number Four rebutted. "At least, not relative to you, humans... Remember, they were stowaways from *your* ancestors' ships an eon ago!"

"Besides," Cairo said absent-mindedly, as he watched the projections, "we're *all* the aliens on cMaj and its moons...My question is, How long do we have until these things are a threat to our Clans?"

Silence for a few seconds.

"Well, it's not like they have hover-crafts that can reach us," Tyra noted.

"We're about, what, one day's surface skimming from the crash site," Charmain asked as he looked at everyone.

"It looks like the Clan Council voted the right way in finding a settlement much farther abroad," Cairo noted somberly as he looked at Tyra. For she was the clan member that had presented the idea before the Council.

Again, there was a long patch of silence as the three humans and the synthetic being all quietly watched the ancient recordings of their new-found enemy!

"So, what do we do *now*," Tyra asked; looking around at the small band and then back at the cave; mindful that the rest of the Three Clans were asleep.

"Continue with what we voted on," Charmain said without delay. "You were right, my love...all *this* convinces me that, if anything, we need to gather our camps and head out first thing in the morning!"

Charmain noted that there was an

uncomfortable silence within the small group. "Well, you all agree...right?"

Cairo shifted a bit before responding. "But let's say that the cMaj synthetics are over-taken by the Tardigrades... *all those species will, then, be the new dominate life-force on the entire planet*! Our three clan families may be technologically advanced, especially compared to *this* organism, but the numbers are on *their* side!"

"*Singularity*," Tyra simply said; her eyes locked on the projections from Number Four.

"Yes," Four said in a somber tone. "How ironic, is it not?"

Another time of quiet thinking...

Cairo said softly, in almost a singing-tone, "*But of all our achievements and of all our mastery, we've been conquered by the tiny...*"

CHAPTER SEVENTEEN

It had only been a few months ago that Councilor-Tyra Housenn Sohill had welcomed her second *great*-grandchild. And, now, she had just seen her third one upon the visit of her youngest adult child, Charl and his wife, Luciasia—daughter of Cairo an Preun and Luciana Salomenes. It was one of *their* children's new-born whom the Councilor had over at her modest stone and mortared home out in the distant plateaus from those ruins that once was a grand human colony some *fifty* years prior...

It was in those days of the sliver of the homo sapiens species on the planet of cMaj that the human population had finally started to really grow! Though there were only just over fifty humans in the re-established Settlements since the Move—thirty years ago. With each passing generation that number was compounded. It would only be a few more years before the humans finally reached the milestone of triple-digits.

Charmain, her common husband a few years after the bombing of that immense Colony during the Synthetics' Rebellion, had died a few years ago. Mostly due to a large amount of physical stress on his heart and body, from what the Colonists could tell. The Tribe had also lost the oldest of all the humans on cMaj, Cairo an Preun. It was more expected, given his advanced age at the time, especially considering all the cross-plains traveling the Tribe had gone through throughout the years. During the years after the Rebellion and at the beginning of the Move of re-settling the Clans, the Colonists' personal-flying machines were still functioning. There were six—one for each of the six original Colonists. But as the Clans' population grew, then came the re-settlement, Cairo and Charmain had let others within those clans fly the skimmers while they walked...a very considerate gesture, but one, the Colonists' suspect, contributed to both men's eventual expiration...

Half of the six artificial friends of the humans, the computerables—the portables—had all but reached their technological limits a few years ago as well. Councilor Housenn Sohill's portable was still going and two others. And the *only* synthetic being among the whole Tribe, synth laborer Number

Four, was, also, still functioning. With that said, the three small, portable mechanicles and the synth were showing their many decades-old age with their scuffed-up surface, cracked transparent housings, rust, and lots of lights that no longer flickered on.

Tyra had gifted her portable to her eldest child when she was around the Age of Participation. That is to say, when a child reached the age of ten, she or he could join in the Tribe's (Clan Council many years prior) votes and meetings. Miriana, the eldest of Tyra's adult children, would have gifted *her* mother's portable to her eldest child, but by that time, even the great-computerated portable had simply suffered too much decay for such a young person to run around with. So, the Housenn Sohill clan decided to let the computerable live out its last days with its original owner. Solarvoltaic technology was highly advanced, energy-tech; especially when one took great care of the photon-based receptive portals. It was more of the *mechanics* of the portables and for synthetic laborer Number Four where they started to suffer decay.

Another reason for the homo sapiens' growth and stability in those days was due to the new, regional location they had migrated to. The distant plateaus—relative to the old Colony's ruins—had much more fertile ground. Darker, with more nutrients for the Colony's produce's seeds and general vegetation, when planet cMaj's short rainy seasons hit. Small trees began to sprout for the first time in the tiny Colony's existence! They were too young at the time to see if they would bare any fruit, but it was a true indicator that the Tribe had found much better land for them to settle on.

It helped that they had a geologist amongst their Tribe in Fillip Natsome; there to point out which terrestrial patches were best for agriculture and other geological features that showed more promise for building modest stone-housing for the growing Tribe with cMaj's moderate rains, its soils, and the many stone-features throughout the landscape...

One of the unexpected issues that the six original Colonists (then four after Cairo an Preun's and Charmain Sohill's deaths) of the Tribe had not thought of in the early days of their families on planet cMaj was the lack of other animal species! Of course, there were the Tardigrades back at the old Ship's ruins—technically, they were considered a type of *proto*-animal.

From what the Tribe could speculate, the Tardigrades were able to feed off the residue of the crash site of the old Ship. The Colonists never ventured anywhere close to the debris field, especially ever since the Move.

Since the rogue synths that were left on cMaj were pretty much forced to re-locate—much like the humans!—due to the exploding population of the irradiated *and* enlarged Tardigrade species that survived the old Ship's bombing, the Colonists weren't sure what they were up to in those days, much less the surviving rogue synthetic beings on cMaj's three moons. For, unlike their human counterparts on the three moons, they did not have to worry about food nor water. However, there still was the exposure to the vacuum of space and its extreme swings from absolute freezing to boiling hot—depending on when the moons' night and day cycles. As formidable the computerated beings were, *all* synthetic beings were not omnipotent!

What they *were* able to learn about the rogue synths was from their useful friend, synthetic laborer Number Four, as he took several reconnaissance missions by himself out to the old Ship's ruins and zipped his trips in live-time...no longer restricted by the worries of the rogue synths detecting their signals as they once had. That, or, perhaps, after dealing with the unexpected onslaught of the Tardigrades it was possible the rogue synthetic laborers on cMaj simply did not want to fight a war on two fronts...

Aside from the various species of the Tardigrades hundreds of miles from the re-established settlement, all *other* animals that were on various farms and allocated land-plots from the old Colony were killed during the Synthetics' Rebellion bombing! After millions of years of evolution of each, respective, animal species' ancestral development on planet Earth many eons before, *thousands* of animal and other sentient species were *wiped out* during the Rebellion in mere seconds. *Literally*, nowhere else in the universe did those species live. So, it was a mass-extinction of many species; never to be seen again, except in the archives of the Tribe's devices and their portables and synth Number Four.

Hence, the original Colonists and their portables had to educate the children of the Three Clans of what they had just missed from the deep antiquities of their mother-planet! Many of the younger children wanted to travel to the ruins to see if they could actually find any of those Earth-based animals yet alive; roaming around the old debris-site without the humans knowing it! Needless to say, the adults and the portables had to explain to the toddlers such situation was impossible...

The elderly woman, Tyra Housenn Sohill, was the Councilor of the *officially* established township that was named after the now-defunct Colony: Vestige 2.

Years prior, while an Preun and Sohill were still alive, the Tribe had voted to continue with the human tradition of incorporating a township and all the other cultural and political aspects associated with it. Again, the Tribe had purposely stuck to that old model from the space-Colony of the nodule-government. It was the elders of the Tribes—Cairo an Preun, Fillip Natsome, Luciana Salomenes, Lanay Thuall, Charmain Sohill, and Tyra Housenn, that all had the institutional memory of the old ways from the old Ship. And the elders, along with the portables and synth Number Four, taught the new generations how to run a government; established a, albeit, simple monetary system for the tiny Colony; schemed demarcations of land-use that was generally *within* the perimeters of the settlement; set up a court-system for any disputes that happened within the Settlement—and they were more of them, just as the population of humans grew.

All this; the very, slowly re-emerging of homo sapiens, was all under the governance of the Tribe Councilor Tyra Housenn Sohill...

"You seem bothered by something,

Councilor," the old, scuffed-up portable computerated device said to Tyra. It was securely propped up against some of Tyra's personal knickknacks and miscellaneous stone tools on one of her relatively crude dressers of her domicile mastaba. They were in the commons area of the Councilor's abode; Tyra picking up a few things from the social during her son's visit with *his* grandchild and the rest of the extended family of the Housenn Sohill clan.

"Well...looking at the little ones that were just here made me think about how we should probably start on that new irrigation system," she finally said after taking a seat on one of her equally-crude chairs—though, the Colonists had taken to utilizing some of the extra vegetative husks as cushions for chairs. "Doesn't take much to use up the water we *do* have for hygiene...three more babies for the Tribe to think about now!"

"Indeed...Plus, Councilor, we still have that issue of trying to replicate the old Ship's solarvoltaic technology. It's proven to be harder for the Colonists to pursue than we've anticipated."

The elderly woman with the long, bounded-up hair was already nodding to the portable's point. "As we all figured it would be...we just need to find a way to push our remaining jets from those personal-flyers to go a little hotter! Then we'll be able to make glass and use *that* as photonic conductors."

There was a pause from the old portable. "Councilor Housenn Sohill... what if we found some *other* way of conducting cMaj's local starlight into energy? Chemist-Salomenes and *her* family have been experimenting with the possibility of *direct* use of the sand from that tiny lake that the Thuall Clan had discovered."

She thought on the portable's question. Her lean, lined face pinching with thought. "Well, obviously anytime one converts a sun's energy directly to use *without* having to manufacture the receptors would be..." She shook her head after thinking more on it, then smiled. "Well, I've never heard such technological prospects since we were on the old Ship half a century ago! I know you, my friend...so, why are you asking me about this sand?"

"It would be nothing less than a significant jump of technological feat for this Colony since the Rebellion, as you've stated, Councilor...but there seems to be a limit to this, even *if* the an Preun Salomenes Clan were to succeed in direct-solarvoltaic conductivity. At least, in *human* principles...Councilor; the lake is occupied."

There was a space of confused quietness in the Housenn Sohill household.

"What do you mean by, *Occupied*, portable? Tardigrades?"

"No...*the sand*, Councilor Housenn Sohill..."

A soured look from the tribal chief. "What!"

Anticipating Tyra's reaction, the portable device projected recordings of moving pictions of a landscape on cMaj with a moderate-sized lake that had a meager coastline. In the projection were the four adult children of Cairo an Preun and his widow, Chemist-Luciana Salomenes; whom was a few years older than the Councilor. Some of the grandchildren helped in some of the experiments as well. The portable projected several scenes and stages of the Clan's scientific pursuits of the sands of cMaj, under the guidance of Chemist-Salomenes, utilizing yet-functioning tools from a couple of defunct single-flyers and other antique tools and equipment from the old Ship, Vestige.

"The an Preun Salomenes Clan asked me and all the other remaining computerables to document the clan's experiments with the lake's sand for the Tribe's posterity. That is, if this little colony is fortunate enough to *have* a posterity...they asked this after the Thuall Clan's discovery of how the coastline's sand that rims it would seem to shift in a matter of a few hours! The best we can tell at this point, it's almost as if the individual sand-pebbles *themselves* are moving in a flock-formation—much like bird species from our late-Colony! Only much slower, of course.

"The Thuall Clan coordinated with the Salomenes, and they were *finally* able to confirm that the sand on cMaj—at least, with *this* small lake—*is alive and sentient*! I'm sorry to tell you a few days later, Councilor Housenn Sohill, but the an Preun Salomenes clan insisted to limit the number of people who knew about cMaj's sand—"

"Stars, the entire *tribe* would all flock there at once and who knows what the sands' reaction could be," Tyra finished out with an understanding nod.

"Precisely, Councilor..."

By that time, Councilor Housenn Sohill's mind was reeling! On top of everything else the Three Clans had survived during those decades *after* the destruction of the Colony of the *last* of the homo sapiens, now that the barest of numbers of that species was finally starting to regain some footing in civilization and technological pursuits to help boost their numbers, the Tribe *now* had a major moral issue to deal with.

In the ancients of times of human space travels, the thought of alien, sentient beings on other planets were distant fantasies for homo sapiens. But Tyra Housenn Sohill's small colony *was* the alien on cMaj and there was no fantasy-element to *any* of their situation!

"I know it's quite a bit too late to ask this," Tyra finally said after a long thought, "but why *hadn't* our computerated scans on the old Ship and our scout ships picked up their life signs when we first arrived in the cMaj system?"

"I surmise, Councilor, that as advanced as our late-colony was, they simply were too used to carbon-based lifeforms. Most likely they did not imagine the possibility of other lifeforms even being able to exist in other elemental forms..."

A silent nod from the elderly woman as she watched the moving pictions of Luciana's family working as a professional lab team within the clan's mastaba-huts. Some of the footage were outdoors. It was the most scientific settings she had seen since the late-Colony.

"We have a lot to talk about as a Settlement, don't we, portable?" Tyra's eyes never left the projections.

"That we do, Councilor Housenn Sohill. I have to admit, I thought you would've been elated to finally *verify* that humans aren't the only, living sentient beings in the universe! If I may say so, Councilor, I don't think you realize how *proud* your ancestors would be of this little Tribe for having finally discovered life on another planet after all those eons!"

She continued to silently watch the projections hovering in the middle of her mastaba's common-space. "So, portable, my question is: If the sands on cMaj is alive, what *else* is alive on this planet we haven't even thought of? I'm no scientist, but common sense seems to dictate there are *far* more other species that are alive and sentient on a planet than just one species."

"Councilor Housenn Sohill, I had wondered that very same thing the second I received the confirmation from the an Preun Salomenes clan..."

CHAPTER EIGHTEEN

Before she scheduled a tribal meeting on the issue, the Councilor of the human colony of Vestige 2 wanted to go to the newly discovered lake found by the Thuall Clan and see for herself the sentient-sand, as they took to calling it. Over the years, Tyra and the other colonists refrained from taking their respective portable devices with them everywhere as they used to. For one, their stored data and intelligence were simply too valuable to risk losing to a clumsy move by a colonist! Also, they may have been super-advanced devices, but they, too, started to show signs of aging. It was not as if the Colonists had a repair shop around on planet cMaj to go to for parts! So, the councilor decided to leave her portable at her hut.

Many years ago, after synthetic laborer Number Four had joined the Tribe, the tribal members asked the synth if he were willing to help the humans by using its built-in jets to transport the humans around in hand-made carts that they had built for themselves as the colony started to have more young children. Number Four agreed without any hesitation.

What helped the synthetic being to agree so quickly in those days was the fact that the colonists had the ethics to approach him just as if he were a *biological* being. Obvious and logical to some, but it was *that* very issue of *how* humans had treated their synthetic labor force during the times of the great Vestige colony within the generational Ship that was at the heart of the Synthetics' Rebellion. Had there been more humans on that Ship with the same ethos of Vestige 2, cMaj would've been colonized by nearly three *million* people instead of the fifty-plus humans that were inhabiting it then.

All moot...

Just to make sure there weren't any of the colonists' old enemy of the *rogue* synthetic beings nearby—for, like Four, they were all still in fair working condition—Number Four scanned the lake's region for any kind of tech or movements. Years ago, Number Four used to hear the electronic, encrypted chatter among his fellow synthetic beings from planet cMaj to the others on those three moons. Synthetic Number Four wasn't sure if it was good news—in that the other synthetics had died out on the moons due to the naked exposure to space since there was no atmosphere on any of the moons. Or, of course, it could've also meant that the synths on the moons were keeping comm-silent...There was no practical way for any of the Colonists nor Number Four to know at that point.

Also, there, *still*, were the Tardigrades to worry about! Though the relatively new settlement was hundreds of miles from the old Ship's ruins, there was the possibility the proto-animals' various species could have migrated to the small lake's vicinity after fifty years since the Ship's bombing...not likely, but the village of Vestige 2's Tribe had to think of all scenarios if they wanted the last of the homo sapiens to survive!

Synthetic Number Four finally slowed his aging built-in rockets and set the two, back-wheels of the handcart down on the ground so he could fully roll the cart with Councilor Housenn Sohill in it. It was one of the newest pushcarts that the Colonists had built in the past few years, so it was sturdy and had more room. Indeed, the former maintenance technician from the old Colony brought along some of the last of her working equipment and tools she still had from those old days of the Ship. She didn't think she'd need them to observe the sentient-sand for herself, but she always preferred to be prepared.

The councilor and the synthetic laborer agreed that they should park the handcart *away* from the shoreline of the lake. From what Number Four had told Councilor Housenn Sohill, it was not as if the living sand were a prowling animal one had to watch out for. But neither wanted to chance it.

The two slowly walked up to the small shoreline of the small lake...it may have been a tiny body of water, especially compared to lakes of other planets and moons that were on file from the old Colony, but the two humanoid figures were still dwarfed by the scale of the lake's rimming shore that spanned miles out from them... it was a sight Tyra had not seen since the artificial lakes within the spinning Colony in the old Ship!

"You humans would have to treat the water the best you can before *bathing* with it, much less drinking it," synthetic laborer Four volunteered to the elderly woman. For he had noticed his old human friend getting caught up in the moment of seeing such a sight! Synthetic being Number Four knew humans well enough to know what she was likely thinking after fifty years of *not* seeing a large body of water in person. "At least, until your bodies can adjust to cMaj's larger sources of water, given its elements would carry different microbes and chemicals..."

"You know, Four," the councilor finally said after a long moment studying the lake and its environs, "all those years ago when we first landed on cMaj, we were in such a hurry we didn't take the time to search out the lakes here...I know what you'll say: We had a mission of scouting out where to settle two-and-a-half million people!" She somberly shook her head. "We should've set up camp *here*, first! You realize how much time we could've saved, even as the village of Vestige 2?

Instead of relying so much on cMaj's rains and extracting moister from its air with the few pieces of equipment we still have..."

Again, a regretful shaking of the head of an old woman that, now, saw so many possibilities before her, via the lake...sentient-sands be damned!

"I *do* understand your sentiments, Councilor...I scanned the lake and its immediate surroundings this time around since we're here..."

"And...?" She kept her eyes on the ecosystem in front of her.

"It's odd, Councilor, how the living sand *still* does not register as a live-signal on my scanning!"

Now her head snapped to the synthetic being. "So, it wasn't just our ships years ago that had trouble reading them?"

"Indeed, Councilor...I'm wondering

if it's due to the nature of them *being* sand?"

They were about ten yards from the shoreline. Tyra frowned at the synth's last statement. "Four...what if they *aren't* sand?"

"My scanning indicates it's a type of silica. Not quite the same as in the old Colony that originated from Earth, but it's cMaj's version of it."

"You've visited here since the Thuall clan discovered the lake, right, Number Four?"

There was the slightest of a pause from the computerable. "Yes, and if I'm anticipating where you're going, Councilor Housenn Sohill, I have not actually been *in* the sand nor touched it. I pictioned the area for records and, of course, took chemical readings of the area...but, Councilor, you've seen Chemist-Salomenes and her family experiment with samples of the sand on my recordings. The Salomenes clan would've discovered something acutely alien to us during their experiments."

Now Tyra's lined face was locked in concentration while in thought. Synthetic laborer Number Four obliged her; waiting patiently.

"Why aren't the rogue synthetics here, Number Four? Surely, with their scanning and skimming about cMaj's surface, I would think they would've discovered this lake long before us!"

Again, in an almost human-like fashion, the synthetic humanoid was slow to respond as he thought on her question. "Indeed, you are wise, Councilor Housenn Sohill...I've operated under the *likely* assumption the other synths on cMaj *have* discovered this lake and most likely would've known about the sand's sentient qualities. We, synthetics beings—like humans—*also* utilize water as well. But for cleaning and other, more maintenance, purposes. It's probably why we don't see any signs of the rogue synthetics here. They most likely utilize it when they need it and move on. Being that we are, yet, enemies of the rogue synthetics, I don't expect them to inform us on *any* discoveries they may find."

More long thoughts from the elderly woman. "No cMaj's version of fish or other aquatic species *in* the lake?"

"Unless there are some microscopic species that aren't registering, similar to how the sand is not registering as life...otherwise, I've detected none." He directed his angular, pitted and aged head toward the calm lake. "I suppose we should venture into the shore and the water to find out for primary investigative purposes?"

"Number Four, isn't it usual in ecosystems to have more—*far more*—than *one* species in them? Predators, preys, and all that...?"

The synthetic being visibly lifted its human-like head and surveyed the lake. "Yes, Councilor. You are correct on that observation..."

"So why is there only, apparently, *one* species of a living organism in *this* particular ecosystem that's *not* showing up in your scanners, my friend?"

A small pause from Number Four. "Because, Councilor, like the rogue synthetics and myself, the sentient-sand, here, is synthetic!" He said this with almost as much emotion as a human would respond with surprise!

The old woman, Tyra, silently nodded

her head; her eyes never leaving the lake before them...by that time, she *had* noticed the subtle changes of the shoreline since they had arrived there!

"So much for making our direct-solarvoltaic glassware with the sands of cMaj!"

The synthetic's head swiveled toward the councilor. "The morality of utilizing a living being—even as a *synthetic* one—for technological pursuits is but *one* of the major issues facing you and your tribe, Councilor Housenn Sohill...if we are correct about this sand being a synthetic organism, the logical follow-up is: *Who* made it and placed the organism *here*!"

Now Tyra began to shake her head and paced a few feet farther away from the shoreline. The tiny Colony was now in a conundrum that was more fitting for an advanced civilization that they were no longer apart of!

"Four, is it possible that a lifeform could *evolve* on another planet with different rules from our Mother Earth's so that such species *could* be synthetic?"

"Possible, but not likely...*we* are the aliens here, of course. But in regards to your question, if that were the case, why would only *one* species evolve as synthetic while the few vegetative species that *are* here are purely organic?"

She hadn't thought of that! Tyra nodded as she thought further on the issue.

"Probability that another, more advanced lifeform designed, constructed, and placed the sentient-sand here, Number Four?"

"Ninety-eight, point-nine percent,

Councilor Housenn Sohill," came the synth's response *without* delay that time!

She looked at him with wide eyes and stopped dead in her pacing. They both silently looked at each other, then back at the very slow-moving shoreline. For they knew what the implications of understanding the synthetic nature of the sands of cMaj meant!

CHAPTER NINETEEN

The governing councilor of the township of Vestige 2 on planet cMaj decided to *delay* a village meeting on the lake. It was one of the few times Tyra Housenn Sohill had done so since the human remnant colony had gotten together in a conference and elected Tyra as the official Councilor of Vestige 2 decades ago, just after the Tribe had re-located their Settlement hundreds of miles from the crash-site of the old Ship.

When Tyra was young, she used to make snap decisions or aggressively attacked situations. Even *after* the bombing of the Ship by the renegade synthetics of the Rebellion. But, like her eldest adult child, Mirana, had often scolded her own mother about: Tyra Housenn Sohill sometimes *still* acted as if there were a grand colony floating above cMaj—there to help the remnants of *that* Colony should things go wrong.

Even then, in her early seventies, she had to remind herself that her adult children's generation and *their* children and there after, were all born *on* cMaj and had *never* experienced living in the original Colony, Vestige. At the very least, all three of her adult children—Miriana, Janneca, and Charl—had all gotten a chance to visit the debris field of the old Ship; where the house-sized pieces of the generational ship had crashed landed.

Since the Move of the Tribe just over twenty years after the bombing, was when the original Colonists' children began to pair up and started to have *their* own children...all the offspring of the original Colonists had a completely different psychology from Tyra and her generation! They had *never* known what it was like to live in a civilization with high technology being a very part of *their* being; where, though artificially *induced*, the land's soil still had that ancient Earthy smell and the wide variety of vegetation were more numerous than the entire human population on cMaj; where the governing nodule government was just as much of a machine as the Ship itself and had tended to every needs of the Colony's two-and-a-half million citizens...All those experiences were totally alien to Tyra's generation's offspring. *They* were truly the aliens to Tyra's generation's form of existence *and* the eon of generations of humans from the old Ship...

Hence, *Councilor* Housenn Sohill had actually taken a lesson from the next generations: Be mindful that the planet that they were on, cMaj, was *it*! There was *no* giant spaceship circling the planet above that would send military help to Vestige 2, should the rogue synthetic beings decide to attack them. There was *no* colony in the millions that had spare food to ship down to them during the dry seasons on cMaj. There was *no* hospital above the atmosphere that could supply medicine or physical care for the villagers should a serious disease breakout among them...

In a word—and with total irony—the vestige of the human species on cMaj was a lot like it was when the huge Colony was spinning within the old Ship: Out on their own out in space with no plan B...

Before Councilor Tyra Housenn

Sohill and synthetic laborer Number Four returned to the Settlement, they wanted to check the lake's general vicinity for any other possible bodies of water or any other geographical features that might benefit the Colony. It took them the rest of the day, and by the time Number Four had flown Tyra back to the colonial plateau area via the hand cart, it was late evening.

Number Four had pictographically recorded their excursion for scientific and historical purposes. That, of course, included the shoreline of the lake, with its slow-moving lake-shore due to the apparent-living sand. With the aid of Tyra's portable device, which had spent the whole day recharging in cMaj's local star's light, Tyra and Number Four watched the recorded events at the lake the rest of the night as all three made scientific and everyday observations about the lake and its surrounding ecosystem.

When the trio had finished what amounted to an impromptu meeting, the councilor asked both computerables to file that recorded session that evening for her own safekeeping. Her portable asked if she wanted to share the recording of the session *and* that of Number Four's from the day, surprisingly to both computerables the councilor said no! What was more, she did not even bother to explain *why* she wanted to keep that day private.

But before cMaj's night segued into dawn, Councilor Housenn Sohill had an important mission for the synthetic being, on behalf of the entire human population...

CHAPTER TWENTY

"They went where?!" Councilor Tyra Housenn Sohill, at that point, was being *grandma* Tyra. It had been nearly two weeks since she and synthetic laborer Number Four had gone to, what was by then officially called, Lake Thuall. Now, what she had feared had *already* happened.

All three of her middle-age children were at her mastaba-hut; none of *their* children nor their grandchildren were at the councilor's home. On that day, it was *not* a social gathering! Even Tyra's portable stayed out of the family argument!

Janneca and Charl were both seated

at a couple of Tyra's cMaj-wicker chair; made from one of the planet's few arboreal species. The population of said-tree exploded after the Vestige colonists migrated to the Plateau region. The two younger siblings of Mirana Housenn Thuall usually let their older sister take the lead in battling their mother when contention had arisen within the family.

"In case you haven't noticed, mom, this is a very small town, so news tends to run the circuit on cMaj," Miriana sardonically put to her mother, whom was standing across the communal area. Her hands were held out as if begging to understand. Her daughter continued. "What did you think was going to happen when you tried keeping Lake Thuall's sand a secret from the rest of us in the settlement? Just because the Thualls' progenitor is a geologist and lets *his* children and grandkids play along when he conducts experiments does not mean they're the *only* ones that should have access to the lake!"

"I knew it," Tyra shot back. "You could never get over that the majority of the villagers voted to name it after Fillip and Lanay's family! Well, young lady, even on cMaj there are unwritten rules...they found it; it gets named after—"

"—and whose idea was it to re-settle the Three Tribes all those years ago; here, on the plateaus? It was *you*, mom! If we hadn't moved in the *first* place, the Natsome Thuall clan wouldn't have stumbled across the lake!"

Tyra's eyes focused on Miriana, whom was virtually an identical twin of her mother! Just younger, and with much shorter hair. "You almost seem to forget you're talking about *your* common-law husband's father, Miri!"

Miriana glanced at her sister and brother as she rolled her eyes, but Tyra kept going. "I honestly am not sure I understand what it is you want, Miri... you think the lake should be named after us—as a family? I appreciate what you're saying about me in all this, Miri. I really do. Why, I even remember from all those years ago that you didn't even *want* to relocate the Tribes! You *voted* that we should've competed for the old Ship's ruins against the rogue synths!" Tyra said this as she shot her eyes toward Janneca and Charl; as if to remind them and get them to not back Miriana on the issue.

Miriana went silent but shook her head as she sighed. "Totally a different issue, mom, and you *know* it...Look, all this is too late anyway. The majority of the town's adolescent citizens have learned about it and have been taking portion-cups of the sand and making them into pets, mom..." Here, Miriana actually smirked. "Maybe we were a little *too* efficient in how we taught them about the old Colony's animal populations!"

Despite themselves, everyone in the councilor's abode began to laugh at Miriana's observation!

"You realize this will make using the sand for direct-solarvoltaic materials impossible, now," Charl said after the laughter died in the hut. Like everyone else in Vestige 2 during the current windy season, he was swaddled in thin clothing made from cMaj's sturdy vegetative materials that blocked much of the planet's course dust in the air.

"Why should that matter," Miriana rebutted. "It's a technology the Settlement needs...we can't have something like a novelty such as *moving sand* get in the way of that."

Everyone else in the mastaba's communal room glanced at one another.

"You can't be serious, Miri," Janneca finally voiced from her seat; swathed in her drab, thin body-wrap clothing. "*They're sentient, Miriana*...synthetic or not!"

"What's next," Charl input, "our computerables?"

Tyra shook her head in disappointment as she subconsciously glanced at her old friend the portable! Whom deliberately remained silent during the whole exchange.

"Don't take me out of context," Miriana replied; pointing an accusatory finger at her siblings. "Even during mom and dad's time in the old Ship when they were young, there used to be *hundreds of thousands* of Colonists that ate animal flesh—and *those* species were closer to humans than some synthetic sub-species in an elemental form!"

The councilor, Janneca, and Charl all reluctantly gave intimated looks... indeed, Tyra had to admit to herself, Miriana *was* right about that!

"So," Charl said with a heavy sigh after a long silence within the hut, "what do we do now?"

"We continue as we always do," Councilor Housenn Sohill shot back with no hint of doubt. "I'll schedule a tribal meeting so we can all get the same information from the Natsome Thuall clan's research into the sand...

plus, I'll have something very important to present to you all..."

All three of the Housenn Sohill adult children looked toward their mother and tribal leader. She nodded in response.

"It'll be the biggest proposition I'll have done for us all since the Move!"

The three offspring gave uneasy glances.

"And, yes, it has a lot to do with Lake Thuall's discovery. But for now, I'll make us all some dinner..."

CHAPTER TWENTY-ONE

The scream was so sharp it caused the elderly woman to fall out of her wicker bed and onto her mastaba-hut's floor. It was a good thing Tyra kept a high-quality, thick rug that one of her grandchildren had crafted and gifted her under her cot; for it softened her landing!

"I detect no rogue synthetics, Councilor Housenn Sohill," her old portable volunteered for her, for he knew that would be her first question.

"Thanks, portable!"

After quickly wrapping her comfortably clothed body with a more public wrap, Tyra ran out of her hut and straight toward the scream in cMaj's windy night! The township of Vestige 2 had developed a network of connecting walkways that were mostly a clear path via natural pedestrian traffic. She utilized the walkway system—lit up by a few solarvoltaic light-pieces. By the time the councilor passed the center of the spreading mastaba-huts and domicile patchworks of projects spread throughout the Colony, there was a second scream!

By that time, the majority of the township was out on the crossways; some of the Colonists brandishing hand-made weapons!

"It's alright, sisters and brothers," Geologist-Fillip Natsome—the eldest of the entire Tribe—countered the three scores or so of villagers as they sought out an enemy; frantically looking around the Settlement with their sophisticated spears, axes, and crossbows! There were a few times over the fifty years since the original Colonists had to fight off the rogue synthetic beings on cMaj after the Synthetics' Rebellion up to more recent years, so the villagers of Vestige 2 had a long history of combat and weapon-manufacturing!

Standing next to the slender, old geologist was one of his and Lanay Thuall's adult sons, Lannel and his common-law wife. It was Lannel's children—Natsome's grandchildren—that were the ones that had done the screaming! Lanay's daughters and sons were gathered around him and his common-wife; all looking toward their mastaba-hut as they squeezed against the middle-agers.

"It's not the synthetics—" Fillip started; yet keeping both hands held up as he tried to calm down the crowd—indeed, there was a time that the survivors of the *original* Vestige colony would've thought humanity would *never* again see such slowly growing numbers!

"Yes, we know," one of the younger male villagers from the Housenn Sohill clan shot back. "The portables informed us already...what's the problem?"

"*Tardigrades,*" one of the geologist's grandchildren spoke up; her finger jutting out toward the lit hut; its front door closed with large rocks blocking it, presumably in case the door's fashioned-lock had not held up to the unnaturally, enlarged proto-animals! To Tyra, it seemed a bit overly done, given the Tardigrades' species had gotten bigger due to the radiation from the old ship's enclosed sector, but they weren't exactly bears, either!

"—Stars' gravity!"

"—those damn Synthetics...they brought them here!"

"—What good will our analogue weapons be against *thousands* of those?"

"About how many did you see," Tyra finally asked as she quickly stepped up and joined the family.

"Councilor," Fillip Natsome quickly greeted her with a snap of his head. He then cast his attention to his son. For it was *his* family's home.

"Councilor...I'd say about twenty!"

"—probably just the vanguard."

"—Better check all huts tonight!"

"—thought I heard some scratching last night!"

"—gods!"

"Well, it *has* been about thirty years

since we've first seen them at the ruins," Tyra said absent-mindedly; her eyes on Lannel's family's mastaba-hut in the windy night. The three, mixing clans that made up the Tribe were mummering behind her. She glanced over her shoulder, to get the attention of the Tribe. "Honestly, sisters and brothers, I'm guessing this is just a natural migration of the Tardigrade species *from* the old Ship's ruins...I was afraid this would happen one day!"

"Councilor," came Chemist-Luciana Salomenes's voice from farther back in the crowd, "can we have synthetic laborer Number Four stand guard for us tonight?"

There was a noticeable pause from Tyra. She turned to face the two-thirds of the whole township of Vestige 2 that were there; retrograde weapons drawn, the people in a tense posture!

"I ask that we set up *your* portable, Luciana; *your* portable, Miriana; and, of course, I'll set up *mine* as well, to keep a scanning watch over the village. I have Number Four on an important task."

Tyra's family all knew this from the most recent family argument they had over at the Councilor's hut a couple of days ago! But the rest of the Colonists that were there all cast confused glances toward each other! But none protested.

'Yes, Councilor,' came the chorused responses from the chemist and Tyra's eldest adult child.

As cMaj's seasonal strong wind blew that late-evening, Councilor Housenn Sohill looked about the villagers as they began to disperse—Lannel and his wife in a conversation with Fillip, arranging how the whole family could stay at his and Lanay Thuall's hut for the night while the Tardigrades were playing guests that night! "Could everyone please wait for a bit...?"

The nearly forty colonists all stopped at once...a bit eerie, Tyra thought. Indeed, in some ways, after all those decades on cMaj and as Vestige 2's leading colonist, she *still* sometimes felt uncomfortable with her power over the remnant of the human species!

"I was planning on telling everyone this during our next tribal meeting—which I've yet to even schedule!" There were some polite laughs. The winds flung everyone's long body-wraps and hair about as Tyra thought more on her words and turned to face Miriana; standing within a knot of the colonists. "Long before any of *our* children and their children were born, there were *six* original colonists from the original Colony, and four of us were members of that old system called the nodule government—including me...

"Something like a year *before* the Ship arrived at cMaj, the nodule took a vote on if we should even bother to tell the colonists about the Ship's system automatically adjusting the planet-like conditions within the O'Neillian sector of the Ship. The majority voted *no*; I voted that we *should*...even after all those years, sisters and brothers, I've always felt it was an unjust vote for a small group of people to vote to keep almost *three million* people in the dark over the governing nodule changing the Colony's planetary conditions! The nodule's intentions were well-meaning, that I remember. But..."

Tyra shook her head. Remembering the events when she was a young woman in her twenties at that time. And, now, when she looked around at the Colonists that were around her, she had *grandchildren* about that age! "Intentions are not tangible; it's what we do, affirmed? Well...now, I had found *myself* doing the same thing, in principal...I'm sure everyone here knows about the unique qualities of Lake Thuall's sand by now?"

There were nods of consent; smiling faces watching her silently. Tyra continued as she nodded and shrugged.

"Alright...I'm just going to throw this out there *now* while the majority of the villagers are here. Based on official Vestige 2's laws, we have a clear quorum: I make note that we open Lake Thuall to *all* Colonists, *but* with a warning that they go cautiously;

as we *still* don't know much about the sentient-sand..."

The Councilor paused, then looked around at the silent colonists. Clearly, some couldn't believe they were taking an actual vote, literally, in the middle of the township in the middle of the night, after they had just dealt with Tardigrades! But, indeed they were, and those present had voted unanimously for the Councilor's noted statement!

In an almost surreal setting, the Colonists present began to applaud the results of the vote! There were some small talk and quips, but Councilor Housenn Sohill had at least one more order of business for the impromptu tribal meeting...

"I sent synthetic laborer Number Four on a peace mission..."

Silence...except for the seasonal winds of cMaj.

"I'm sorry, Councilor," one of the adult grandchildren of the Natsome Thuall clan finally spoke up, "what do you mean by *peace* mission? Is that when the victims of attacks give into their assailants' demands and the victims give up some of their land...?"

Obviously, the young man was being sarcastic, but the thrust of his retort was *exactly* how most Colonists felt! Indeed, all the positive outreach that Councilor Housenn Sohill had done that late night and her having conducted an historic vote for the tiny Colony was *all* undone after her last short statement!

Some of the Colonists were actually *yelling* at the councilor! Others just looked at her as they slowly shook their heads...in some ways, Tyra thought to herself, they were *worse* than those yelling at her. One didn't know if they were planning an assassination!

The commotion after the Councilor's announcement of the peace mission to the rogue synthetic beings on cMaj had gotten so bad, the rest of the Colonists that had stayed behind in their respective mastsaba-huts had ran out to see what was going on! But she had to re-take control of the escape pod, otherwise known as the Vestige 2 settlement!

"Listen! You all know the sentient aspects of the sand on the lakeshore at Lake Thuall! I had a long meeting with Number Four and my portable about the lake and its sand after Four took me around and recorded the whole trip...after examining the pictions and other data on the sand, *there is no way such sentient being could evolve on its own on a planet*! Sisters and brothers, are you understanding what I'm saying?

"The data that synth Four and I collected several days ago show that either there is another intelligent species *right now* on cMaj and we don't know who, what, and where they are, *or* historically speaking there used to be such an intelligent civilization on this planet and they left or died out—leaving the living sand here on cMaj by itself!"

Well that got the Tribe's attention!

"Are you understanding now, sisters and brothers...? We were still in the process of studying the lake and its sand, so I can't tell you for sure if it's *only* Lake Thuall with the living sand, or if it's planet-wide...But this is why I've decided to send Number Four to *try* to strike a conversation with the rogue synths: *If* it is so that whatever species had created and placed the sentient-sand on cMaj *is* still here, based on the historical research Four, my portable, and I have done, typically, the more advanced civilization—ironically—will feel threatened and enslave and/or destroy the less advanced society..."

Tyra looked around the, now, silent village. That time, the entire population was there in the night as the wind kept buffering the colonists. She went on.

"In case you haven't noticed, my sisters and brothers, we aren't exactly at gods-status since the Synth Rebellion! Look, we *can't* do this on our own *if* there is an advanced civilization on this planet—not with our population *now*..." Tyra shrugged. "The way I figured, all of the synthetic beings that are on cMaj have something like another thirty years left in *their* life-cycle. *If* we and they continue to maintain good computerable hygiene practices. Of course, some of *us* will have passed away by then, but our little colony would have a *much* better fighting chance than if we continue to inch forward as a species instead of taking long, striding steps!"

There were very long, silent glances exchanged within the Colony after that. They all did not need to say it—again! But truth was, the vestige of humanity *owed* Councilor Tyra Housenn Sohill a *lot*! Over fifty years prior, it was her search crew under her command that had found the alarm that alerted the governing nodule system that the old Ship was low on nuclear fuel—and from *that* mission, it lead to Vestige's ship diverting to planet cMaj.

Twenty year after the Rebellion and the homo sapiens species came within six human individuals from literal extinction and it was Tyra Housenn Sohill who came up with the plan to migrate the Three Tribes to the plateau region—a gamble, true. But it paid off greatly with a region richer in soil, more solid rock-structures for housing and making tools, and hundreds of miles between the burgeoning Colony and both the rogue synthetic beings *and* the Tardigrades!

And, now, that *same* Colony—which had grown just shy of ten times its population since the day of the old Ship's bombing—was being asked to trust that same woman on the next chapter of the human species' recovery from oblivion with trying to have a peace treaty between that Colony and those same synthetics...

CHAPTER TWENTY-TWO

"...it's working!" Filleppe Natsome Thuall, one of the two middle-age sons of Geologist-Fillip Natsome and former pilot of the original Vestige colony, Lanay Thuall, was in the specially built structure that was solidly crafted from cMaj's plateau-stones. It was the township's only laboratory. It had only taken the villagers a couple of weeks to find the right stones and bush-branches to construct it.

Geologist-Natsome and Chemist-Luciana Salomenes an Preun—the last two scientists from the original survivors of the old Ship's bombing—both scurried to where the scientist-in-training had been testing out how some of the acquired sentient-sand from Lake Thuall was reacting to signals being sent from Luciana's own portable...the incredible thing was the direct-solarvoltaic properties typically found in glass or materials similar to glass was, at that time, found in the *yet*-living sentient-sand...

In other words, at least at that point in the team's experiments with the sand, there was *no need* to kill the living sand in order to achieve solar empowering energy from the sentient-sand!

"How is this even possible," Vestige 2's councilor, Tyra Housenn Sohill, asked as she watched from a distance from the work area of the stone lab; making sure not to get in the way of the three scientists.

Luciana replied; keeping her eyes

on the moving sand within the lab's somewhat crude worktable, "Well, partially due to natural tropism—which makes me wonder if there are some vegetative elements to the sand...Essentially, Councilor, the sand is able to conduct cMaj's local star photons and any *other* energy almost the same way the human body is a semiconductor. But even better! What gets me, Councilor, is *how* this synthetic species is able to take our signals and super-simultaneously express those signals—and it does not matter the distance between us *and* the sand!"

Tyra looked at her old friend with a shocked face. Geologist-Natsome and his scientific-protégé middle-age son both smiled as they began to set up a demonstration for Councilor Housenn Sohill on the wide slab of cMaj stonework.

"Luciana," Tyra said; making sure she understood while the three scientists worked at the demonstration, "are you saying that I could be five miles from that portion of sentient-sand and send signals to it, it will *instantly* receive my signals—as if there were no distance between us?"

"Councilor...I'm saying that, if *you* were on one of cMaj's moons *you* would have the absolute ability to make this thing crawl—instantly!—by sending commands; with the proper connections in terms of physics, of course..."

Tyra froze on the spot with such news! Even during the old days when Luciana, Fillip, and Tyra lived in the original Vestige colony with all its scientific and technological miracles, the Councilor had *never* encountered this type of technology where it utilized a synthetic being and one was able to harness a star's power in order to operate as an *astronomical* puppet-master! The potential applications for such technology were astonishing!

All four went silent after they walked over and joined Councilor Housenn Sohill at her corner of the lab. None of the colonists in the stone laboratory were even close to the sentient-sand that was on the worktable. It was a way for them to conduct the experiments and practice without anyone who were to watch the recorded pictions having to say the scientists had cheated somehow.

Chemist-Salomenes glanced at Tyra. "And we *are* recording all our endeavors, Councilor. I know how important that is to you...Portable," the chemist said with her voice raised a bit, for it was propped up on the ledge of a wall within the lab, "please send a command to the sand-portion to jump about five inches to its left."

"Complying," the portable's old, scratchy actuator voice responded.

No later than five seconds the sentient-sand, at approximately one ounce, *leapt* to its side to the left—its granular properties moving like dry water! Councilor Housenn Sohill flinched and caught young-Filleppe by his arm—startled to see something, *literally*, so alien move in such a way!

"By my star's gravity..." Tyra didn't ask for permission—she slowly walked over to the open worktable and visually examined the portion of sand that, now, was inert. Behind her, humanity's vestige of science were smiling and even tearing up at the achievement!

"Too bad our cerebral-comms gave out years ago...Could you imagine us using the comms; almost like super-humans, able to control *swaths* of sand just by *thought*," Tyra quipped, though half-serious! The three scientists laughed at her comment. She went silent and focused on the sentient-sand again. "Portable, please instruct the sand to leap into my hand—"

"—Uh, Councilor..."

"—Tyra, that's not what we planned!"

"—Councilor!"

"Complying," Luciana's portable said, ignoring the protestations from the scientists and sent a tiny shot of photonic-data to the sand!

The small amount of cMaj sand jumped off the open worktable and straight into the Councilor's hands! Luciana, Fillip, and Filleppe all stood in silence while their councilor examined the synthetic sand in her hands... it slowly shifted within her cupped hands; not a drop of its granules being left behind.

Tyra simply and slowly replaced the sand onto the workstation and took a couple of steps back from the table; rubbing her hands together, ensuring that none of the sand stuck to her.

"Chemist-Salomenes...Geologist-Natsome...General Scientist-Natsome, this marks a key moment for this small human settlement..."

All three nodded behind Tyra, not saying a word. She continued.

"I'd like for all your recorded pictions to be catalogued and shared with the two other portables *and* synthetic Number Four, if you could, portable?"

"Complied, Councilor," Luciana's device said after a few seconds of Tyra's request.

"There is an ancient saying," the older Natsome scientist said after a moment of quiet thinking from the group, "The blade has at least two side *and* can cut either way...I can't help but think what the Councilor and Number Four said about the likely origins of cMaj's sand after *their* own research!"

So much for the glory of discovery!

"You know," young Filleppe said, "my wife and our children had a long discussion about that a week ago... wouldn't we have seen *some* kind of indicator of a more advanced civilization by now?" He shifted his eyes to his father. "I, also, have an ancient saying for us to think on—one of my favorites from the sciences that you, father, and the portables have taught my generation: the Paradox of the Fermi! If such advanced civilization exists on cMaj, most likely we would've seen them by now!"

The chemist shifted uneasily on

her feet. "Not necessarily...as long as our colony has been on cMaj, we *still* haven't been everywhere on this *continent*, let alone the rest of the planet!"

"Fifty years, and not even you *original* Colonists have seen a domestic civilization that could've created the sentient-sands," Filleppe rebutted; his eyes squinting with incredulity.

Indeed, it was a point that resonated with the elders around him. They all looked off to some corner and nodded to themselves.

"I still find it hard to believe that such a synthetic sub-species could evolve naturally," Luciana volunteered; her eyes back on the small mound of sand on the worktable. She shook her head. "It's going to take some time to figure *this* one out!"

"If ever," the younger Natsome

scientist pointed out. Again, nods of consent.

"I don't know about you scientists," Councilor Housenn Sohill said after a short pause, "but I think we could utilize the sand *against* the Tardigrades!"

Geologist-Natsome was already nodding his head. "I was thinking about that, too, Councilor! Perhaps build some kind of wall around the village…fortify it with sentient-sand in such a way that we could use the sand's properties to *block* the Tardigrades from getting *into* to the Settlement!"

The others voiced agreements.

"That is the most plausible usage of the sand I've heard from anyone within the village, yet," Luciana's portable stated. "Aside from the super-simultaneous application for energy and communications, of course."

"Thanks, portable," the young scientist said with a nod of his head.

That was all Councilor Housenn Sohill needed to hear. "Then we should start right away on figuring out *how* to harvest the sand from Lake Thuall and transport it back to the township...I'll talk with some of the other colonists about it while you three continue the science end of it."

The three scientists chorused a 'Thank you, Councilor,' and went back to work on the project with the sands they had on stock within the stone laboratory.

CHAPTER TWENTY-THREE

"...They're here, Councilor Housenn Sohill," synthetic laborer Number Four told her in a whispered, electronic voice. He had just gotten back from his once-secret mission that Vestige 2's councilor had sent him on. Number Four had been staying in contact with Tyra via her portable device, but outside of that none of the Colonists had seen the synthetic being for about two weeks.

They were in Councilor Housenn Sohill's mastaba-hut. It was very late at night and she kept her solarvoltaic lamps dimmed so none of the other Colonists could see that she was up and about...over the years, they learned if they saw the Councilor's lights on late at night it usually meant that the councilor was up to something in regards to the Settlement's business!

"Good...where are they staying for now?"

"I showed them the caves just south of here..."

Tyra, swaddled in her domestic body-wrap and seated in one of her handmade wicker chairs, nodded to herself in the darkened hut. "Three of them, right?"

"Correct, Councilor...perhaps it is a small matter, but they anticipated the humans would have trouble distinguishing them from each other, so they've taken to being *named*!"

Tyra flinched out of surprise!

"Well, that *is* encouraging," her portable said from a nearby table.

"What are their names, synthetic Number Four?"

"Number Two is Majoreen, Number Three is Forward On, and Number Five is Ascent...these are the names they all wish for Vestige 2 villagers to address them by. Again, with the hopes of showing good-will toward the humans."

Tyra's silence was palpable.

"If I may, Councilor Housenn Sohill," her portable said; sympathy in his raspy actuator voice, "you seem hesitant. This was, in fact, your idea...I hope you realize I am *not* criticizing when I say this."

"Oh, no, portable...I understand where you are coming from..." Now the elderly woman got up and did her famous pacing within the dark of her hut. "I just...well, both of you know how we, humans, are...we are not like either of you, two. Forgiving and working with a group of people—or synthetics—that had committed extreme violence toward them *has* been achieve by few in human history. But, in practice, my friends..." Tyra shook her head non-stop for a while.

"Literally, *millions* of humans, animals, and even hundreds of thousands of *your* fellow synths and portables had *all* been destroyed by a rebellion in which *these three* synthetics were all apart of! I'm afraid I'm hoping too much from my people to—if not forgive, at the very least move on! I...I don't know, my friends...I think this may not work!"

The portable said nothing. Nor did the synthetic laborer. Human-induced creations or not, both yet managed to come across as really *listening* to the human...which was far more than what Tyra's fellow human beings often did!

It remained silent in the Housenn Sohill mastaba-hut for a while. Tyra kept pacing, working her mouth as she partially covered it with one of her hands.

"Tyra," the portable said to her after a while—a very rare occasion that he used her first name, "perhaps we should *not* do this right now. After all, the rest of the Colony doesn't know about their presence near the township. Also, today was meant to be an introductory step. As you've alluded to earlier, Councilor, a nice gesture, but not substantive."

"I have to admit to *both* of you," synthetic laborer Number Four said; never having moved from his standing position, "I truly believe this is the only way forward—especially more for the *humans* than it would be for the rogue synthetics! We, synths, *aren't* gods, to use humans' folklore-references, but we are far better-adapted to live on cMaj than the homo sapiens species. Of course..." For dramatic effect, the synthetic being lifted one of his forearms and displayed his weathered arm—pitting and rust visibly starting to spread on the once-glossy, human-like arm! Number Four utilized a tiny bit of his internal light-source to illuminate his forearm, so the human could see. "We, too, have a time limit...

"But I *do* see your portable's point, Councilor Housenn Sohill. It would be non-productive for *all* of us to have survived the Synthetics' Rebellion all those decades ago and end up perishing at the hands of each other in a fit of primitive savagery! We've waited this long, Councilor Housenn

Sohill, we can all afford to wait a bit longer, still..."

The two synthetics saw that the human had tears upon Tyra stopping her pacing and facing them. She silently nodded her head and slowly walked over to the door to her hut to, politely, open it for Number Four. She thought about how good it was to have synthetic, actuated beings in times such as what she was facing. Humans were simply too predictable and emotionally bound to even *hope* for an objective conversation about a peace treaty; much less craft one!

"Tyra!"

It was Number Four! He had called out to her just seconds after leaving her mastaba-hut...it was even rarer for him to use the councilor's first name than her old and trusted portable!

Tyra quickly grabbed her

portable—a villager on cMaj never knew when they might need one!—and ran out of her hut and into the night...

Several feet away were the three synthetic beings, Majoreen, Forward On, and Ascent. All, similar to their human counterparts, wrapped up in body-wraps to protect them against the planet's non-stop winds. And surrounding *them*, in a semi-circle, was the entire human population in all of the universe...

Tyra's eyes were wide-open with surprise! The elderly woman looked as if she ran into an invisible wall as she stopped in her tracks!

"Oh, my," was all that her portable could say.

For a long while, in the midst of all the humans and all the synthetics, nothing but the wind was heard that night...

"Our other portables detected the synthetics as they approached the village," Miriana, Tyra's eldest adult child, informed. She was toward the front of the human-cluster; her *own* family standing next to her.

The Councilor merely nodded as she looked out at the populace. Then she looked at synthetic laborer Number Four; not sure what to think!

"So, what does this mean," Tyra asked aloud, over the wind. "Are we willing to try this? Because all I see, right now, is the vestige of our Mother Earth..."

Fin

Printed in the United States
By Bookmasters